SURRENDER TO
HER SPANISH
HUSBAND

With grateful thanks to my lovely editor
Sally Williamson.
Her gentle guidance and support help
make my part of the deal a joy!

He froze. She must be dreaming, he thought. But then she laid her hand across his cheek, tenderly stroking it. 'You're such a good man really...and sometimes... sometimes so hard to resist.'

'Do you know what you are saying?' he demanded huskily.

'Yes, I do. I'm wide awake, Rodrigo.'

'This is a dangerous game you're playing, Jenny Wren.'

'Don't you want to kiss me?' she whispered, her hand moving gracefully from his cheek into his hair.

His blood heating violently, Rodrigo gripped her shoulder. Self-control was suddenly frighteningly thin. 'I want much more than just a sweet, drowsy little kiss, my angel. Unless you are prepared for that then we will stop this right here, right now.'

In answer, Jenny gazed up at him with her bewitching light eyes full of longing, and then with a fleeting bold smile she slanted her petal-soft lips against his.

The day **Maggie Cox** saw the film version of *Wuthering Heights*, with a beautiful Merle Oberon and a very handsome Laurence Olivier, was the day she became hooked on romance. From that day onwards she spent a lot of time dreaming up her own romances, secretly hoping that one day she might become published and get paid for doing what she loved most! Now that her dream is being realised, she wakes up every morning and counts her blessings. She is married to a gorgeous man, and is the mother of two wonderful sons. Her two other great passions in life—besides her family and reading/writing—are music and films.

SURRENDER TO HER SPANISH HUSBAND

BY
MAGGIE COX

MILLS & BOON

First published in Great Britain 2010
Harlequin Mills & Boon Limited,
Eton House, 18-24 Paradise Road, Richmond, Surrey TW9 1SR

© Maggie Cox 2010

ISBN: 978 0 263 21412 3

Harlequin Mills & Boon policy is to use papers that are natural,
renewable and recyclable products and made from wood grown in
sustainable forests. The logging and manufacturing process conform
to the legal environmental regulations of the country of origin.

Printed and bound in Great Britain
by CPI Antony Rowe, Chippenham, Wiltshire

CHAPTER ONE

An ear-splitting bolt of lightning shrieked through the air, lighting up the interior of the house's cosy hallway and outlining in threatening shadow the figure that loomed up behind the door's decorative stained glass panels. Her foot on the first tread of the stairs, on her way up to the hot scented bath that promised to be the perfect antidote to the day's accumulated stresses and strains, Jenny came to a sudden shocked standstill.

It was almost ten in the evening. There had been no phone call to tell her of the imminent arrival of a guest, and there were no other occupants in the entire place but her. Bearing in mind Raven Cottage's remote, some might say wild location—miles from anywhere—she had to quickly rid herself of the nightmarish scenario that her mind unhelpfully and frighteningly presented her with. But deepening dread paralysed her for long seconds before she could shake it off.

Installed as temporary caretaker of the charming thatched-roof guesthouse for nearly three full months now, courtesy of her friend Lily, who had gone to visit her parents in Australia, in all that time Jenny had not once chafed against her isolated surroundings at all. If anything, its lonely proximity to the Atlantic Ocean had given her a chance to properly take stock of all that had happened. Bit by bit she'd been rebuilding her esteem.

Divorce was never easy, but hers had been reluctant and sorrowful. She still ached for what might have been if her ex-husband hadn't rent her heart in two by deciding he could no longer continue with the marriage. Even though that had been years ago, from time to time Jenny still reeled from it. Standing out at the water's edge sometimes, she'd stare at the colossal waves sweeping into the shore and they seemed to symbolise the emotional battering she had taken. And If the divorce hadn't been traumatic enough fate had then delivered another blow—one that that had been particularly cruel.

But maybe it was because it was such a stormy 'end of the world' kind of night that her imagination seemed intent on putting her centre stage into a scene straight out of a horror movie…the kind that made her wonder if the people who watched them were altogether sane.

The shadowy figure outside lifted the brass knocker, banging it loudly. The discordant sound was like nerve-jangling rifle-shot, intent on drilling a hole through her skull. Biting her lip, Jenny breathed in deeply.

'Just a minute. I'm coming!' Having raised her voice above the din of a growling roll of thunder she fleetingly wished she'd pretended she wasn't home. Her caller would hopefully have just gone away and she could have enjoyed her longed-for bath in peace. But, knowing Lily needed the business, she plastered on a smile then opened the door.

'*Dios mio!* Could there be a more remote inhospitable place in the world?'

The darkly clothed male figure who, even after only the short sprint from his car, looked as if he'd been swimming in a roiling river, immediately vented his frustration.

Eyes the colour of silken jet pierced Jenny like dangerously sharpened dagger-points. Her determinedly upbeat smile vanished. It had been on the tip of her tongue to burst out *Well, if it's so inhospitable, and you'd rather be somewhere else, why have you bothered to knock on my door?* But the words died in her throat—because her visitor was shockingly familiar.

Eyes widening, she pressed her hand to her chest. 'Rodrigo. What are you doing here?' Her body shivered hard from the blast of freezing air that the opened door brought with it.

Her ex-husband stepped inside, causing Jenny to back up nervously. Shaking his mane of sleekly dark hair, then staring at her with a gaze that deluged her with a sea of haunting memories, he wiped the back of his hand across his damply glistening face. 'I might ask you the same question.'

'I'm looking after the place for Lily while she's away in Australia.' Clearly Jenny's presence was as much a surprise to him as his was to her. The ridiculous hope that he'd sought her out because he wanted to reconcile was cruelly and devastatingly snatched away. Despite her sorrow, she forced herself to carry on speaking. 'Now it's your turn. What brings you to the wilds of Cornwall? I wouldn't have thought it could hold much appeal—especially in the winter. The Mediterranean is much more your style.'

He sighed, as though it pained him to even consider some suitably witty repartee. 'I'm in the area because I have a meeting tomorrow. Have you a room? For pity's sake don't turn me out into that—that violent monsoon again!'

'I'd take pity on anyone who was in danger of being swept away by such wild weather...even *you*, Rodrigo. It's pretty grim out there tonight. Anyway... you're in luck. We're not fully booked. We're actually very quiet at the moment.'

Best not tell him he's the only guest just the same... Unconsciously grimacing, Jenny skirted round her formidably built ex-husband to hastily shut the door against the raging storm.

'Thanks.' Reaching out a hand, he squeezed her shoulder as his well-cut lips formed a lopsided smile. 'It is gratifying to know that you don't hate me enough to leave me to my fate.'

Parrying the nervous heat that flooded her, she backed up again.

'I expect you'd like to go straight to your room? You must be dying to get out of those soaking wet clothes.'

Another inconvenient wave of heat suffused Jenny at the remark she'd made. But she'd been referring to the imminent shedding of Rodrigo's clothes, so it hardly came as a surprise.

'I am. But first I will have to make a dash back to the car to collect my luggage.'

No sooner was this said than done, and once again Jenny was treated to a perfectly icy blast of arctic cold as she waited for Rodrigo to return with his suitcase, and an expensive calf leather shoulder bag that she knew contained a laptop.

'You'd better give me your coat,' she said, making herself wait patiently as he removed his damp trench-coat and then held it out to her. She desperately wanted to present an appearance of composure, even though inside her feelings easily mirrored the violent chaos of the storm.

A fleeting rueful smile touched Rodrigo's lips. 'I don't want to ruin Lily's polished wooden floor-boards,' he remarked.

Hanging the garment on a peg at the back of the door, she saw droplets of icy water from the hem drip rhythmically onto the raffia doormat. 'I'll hang it in the utility room in a little while,' she told him.

The spicy cologne that clung to the material of his

coat made a direct assay into her already besieged senses, causing another disturbing skirmish low in her belly. She frowned, hugging her arms over the lilac wool sweater that she'd teamed with well-worn faded blue jeans. 'So...where's this meeting you've got tomorrow?'

'Penzance. I was booked into a hotel there, but the roads were treacherous in this storm, and my sat nav stopped working. As I was driving I remembered that Lily had a guesthouse somewhere close by. I didn't even have to look for it—that was the crazy thing. Believe it or not somehow the place just loomed up before me... It's a total surprise to find *you* here.'

He hesitated, as if he was going to add something, and Jenny deliberately smothered the persistent ridiculous hope that doggedly had hold of her heart with a pincer grip.

'So you only need a room for the one night?'

'That's right. And what you said earlier was right too...the Mediterranean *is* more to my taste.'

'Then God forbid that you should suffer more than you have to!' she answered waspishly, turning away. Her insides went crazy when Rodrigo caught hold of her hand.

'Do you want to make me suffer, Jenny?' His dark eyes glittered.

Pulling her hand free from his icy cold palm, she dismissively tossed her head. 'I can assure you that I've got far more important things to do with my time. The room's this way.'

She led him upstairs to the luxurious accommodation at the front of the house, knowing that it was
the best room in the building. No matter what had
transpired between them as a couple, she knew he
had faultless good taste—and she didn't want him
to find flaws in her friend's much loved business. In
the morning he would be treated to something pretty
spectacular. When the landscape wasn't shrouded
in mist and dark, or sheeted with blinding incessant
rain, he'd find a view that couldn't fail to stir the
senses and feed the soul. Again—despite her personal feelings—Jenny hoped Rodrigo would appreciate
it.

Artists, writers, honeymooning couples and folk
recovering from illness, divorce or bereavement—
they had all stayed in that room, Lily had told her.
With its unparalleled vista reflecting the Atlantic
Ocean's dramatically beautiful unpredictability, it
was a firm favourite with everyone. And, going by
the comments in the visitors' book, they all swore
that the bewitching and haunting wild scenery had
definitely worked its magic, making them devotees
for life by the time it came for them to leave.

Now, surveying the exotically handsome looks of
the man who had once been her husband as he deposited his stylish suitcase and bag on top of the lovingly
created silk patchwork quilt on the bed, Jenny saw
him glance round the room with little evidence of
pleasure or satisfaction on his face. Didn't he like it?
There was a brooding, disenchanted air about him

that reminded her that he had seen and done it all, more or less, and since there wasn't much that could impress him it was probably a waste of time even trying.

On her friend's behalf, Jenny was affronted. The beautifully presented room, with its plush velvet curtains and matching swags, tasteful designer wallpaper that had cost an arm and a leg, immaculate antique Davenport and sumptuous king-sized bed, complete with bespoke iron bedstead, had taken a large chunk of her friend's savings to perfect. It was a luxurious and relaxing atmosphere, yet at the same time Lily had managed to retain the old-fashioned English charm that the tourists expected and loved. And, being in the business of interior design, Jenny had been happy to advise her.

After the devastating death of Lily's sister and her husband in a car crash, Lily had found herself sole owner of Raven Cottage, and she had become absolutely determined to rise above the terrible tragedy she'd suffered and make the guesthouse a resounding success in their memory.

Like Jenny, Lily was no stranger to the bitter and jolting twists of fate that could cut a person off at the knees. That was why the bond between them that had begun all those years ago at school had deepened even more over the last couple of years.

Just before they had entered the room Jenny had flicked a switch to turn on two small antique table lamps either side of the bed, bathing the room in a softly inviting amber glow. As the rain whipped at the old-fashioned windows, and the crashing thunder overhead literally shook the rafters, she thought it would be hard to find a cosier place to shelter from such primitive violent weather. But again she found herself wondering if her jaded ex-husband even had the capacity to appreciate it.

'So…how come you've got a meeting in Cornwall?' Summoning a determinedly neutral tone, Jenny focused her apprehensive gaze on Rodrigo Martinez— billionaire owner of a chain of spa/hotels that were some of the most exclusive in the world. His carved handsome face, with its deep-set black eyes and spiked ebony lashes still damp from the rain, gave her his full attention. In return, her hungry glance moved helplessly over his arrestingly fit body. A body that suggested a disturbing physicality for which the outer garb of black sweater and jeans was only a thin shield. Rodrigo's simmering sexuality had fascinated and thrilled Jenny right from the beginning.

'I'm opening one of my hotels in Penzance,' he replied, his accent underlined by the husky gravel of his voice. 'Research tells me it's a popular area.'

'So naturally you want to capitalise on it?'

Unoffended, he shrugged. 'I'm a businessman in the hotel trade…what did you expect?'

Jenny's mouth dried with hurt. 'Nothing. I expect nothing of you, Rodrigo. Except maybe for you to act like you've always acted. I learned that lesson a long time ago, remember?'

'And you still bear a grudge towards me for it, by the sound of things.' Sighing, he drove his fingers irritably though his rain-damp hair. 'I need to get out of these wet things and take a hot shower. Unless you're feeling reckless and want to join me, I suggest it's time you vacated my room.'

'Go to hell!' Jenny reacted instantly, her heart suffused with indignant anger as well as painful regret.

'You think I haven't been there before, *querida*?' Shaking his head, his voice low, Rodrigo ruefully dropped his hands to his hips.

'When was that? When you failed to secure some million-dollar deal to make you even richer? That must have been a real low point!'

'What a flattering not to mention *damning* opinion you have of me, Jenny. You think all I'm interested in in life is making money?'

'I don't think that at all.' Her hand curved round the doorknob, Jenny met his disturbing gaze with unflinching steadiness. 'I *know* it.' She would have slammed out through the door there and then if her innate good nature hadn't got the better of her. 'I'll make you some coffee and get you a bite to eat. I expect you're hungry after your long drive. It'll be in the kitchen when you're ready.'

'Jenny?'

'Yes?'

'Nothing…it will keep. We can talk later.'

Bereft of a handy reply, and hardly trusting herself

to speak without becoming emotional, Jenny left the room. In the corridor her footsteps slowed. It had been over two years since she'd seen Rodrigo. She'd foolishly kept hoping he'd ring or get in touch, but he never had. In her mind she'd imagined him saying he'd made a mistake—he'd only asked her for a divorce because he was stressed—he'd been working too hard and hadn't been thinking straight. *No such event had occurred.* When she'd returned to the UK from Barcelona, where they had lived together, Jenny's friends had advised her not to waste any more precious time thinking about him. If he couldn't see the gift he had so easily let go then he just wasn't worth it. Why didn't she just spend the money he'd insisted she take as a divorce settlement, have a good time, and forget him?

As if she was going to wake up one morning and forget how to breathe. Day and night Rodrigo's memory haunted her. Her thoughts seemed incapable of dwelling on much else. But she wasn't happy that he still had the power to affect her so profoundly. She wanted to show him that she'd moved on...made a new and satisfying life without him. But after the pain and mayhem her brother Tim had caused when Jenny had returned to the family home 'new and satisfying' would have been a lie.

Her teeth clamping painfully down on her lip, Jenny headed back downstairs to the kitchen. A violent shudder rolled through her as a flash of lightning eerily illuminated the house's interior. The hall lights flickered wildly. To add to the sticky, uncomfortable tension in the air that shrouded her like a fine cloying mist—despite the arctic temperature outside—she nearly jumped out of her skin when a slightly over-weight, well-fed tabby weaved her way awkwardly round her legs and almost sent her sprawling.

'Cozette, you naughty girl!' Jenny scolded, scoop-ing the purring feline up from the floor and then holding the generous bundle of warm soft fur close into her chest.

She didn't mind admitting that Lily's pet cat had become a very welcome companion during her so-journ in the wilds of Cornwall.

'How many times have I told you not to do that? Never mind, are you scared of the storm? Is that what's bothering you? Poor little kitty…don't worry. I'll take you into the kitchen and find you a nice tasty bite to eat to help take your mind off this terrible racket!'

Upstairs in his room, in the act of retrieving his laptop from its leather holdall and wondering if this Cornish wilderness had even *heard* of the internet, Rodrigo paused. The voice that drifted up to him from downstairs riveted him. *It always had.* Now he stood perfectly still, listening. The lady had a voice as alluringly velvet as a warm midsummer's night, and it wrapped itself round his senses like a soft Andalucian breeze, full of the scents of jasmine, orange and honeysuckle and other exotic flowers that could render one hypnotised by their scent alone.

Hearing Jenny's voice again after being denied the sound for over two years... The effect it had always had on him ricocheted hotly through Rodrigo's brain. *Not to mention other sensitive parts of his body.* As he listened to her croon now, to what he quickly deduced must be Lily's pet cat, the napped velvet tones and cultured British accent were enough to raise goosebumps up and down his forearms and unquestioningly to arouse him. He blew out a breath. *Steady, Rodrigo...*he ruefully warned himself. She was still pretty mad at him, and had every right to be.

They'd been married for just over a year when he'd declared that they must part. Even now he could hardly believe he'd said the words—never mind seen them through. He should definitely rein in the almost instantaneous lust that had all but exploded through him at the sight of her tonight. Those luminous cornflower-blue eyes in a stunning oval face framed by a gilded curtain of shoulder-length blonde hair had always hit him where it hurt. He had never set out to wound her so badly. But—that aside—he had travelled to this spectacularly haunting part of the country for the purposes of business, *not* pleasure. And of all the startling scenarios he might have envisaged on this trip, having his beautiful ex-wife open the door to him on arrival at her friend's guesthouse was not one of them—though he had to admit his spur-of-the-moment plan had been influenced by the hope of hearing news of her.

His heavy sigh was laden with equal parts of frustration and tension. He kicked off his Italian-made shoes and tore off his socks, allowing his long tanned feet to sink gratefully into the luxurious carpet, before stripping off his clothes and heading for the shower...

'Do you have access to the internet here?'

'What? Oh, yes...but the signal's a bit dodgy. I mean, it comes and goes...especially in a storm like this.'

'I feared as much.'

'We'll probably get connected again tomorrow, when things have calmed down a bit. You may as well resign yourself to a night of not working. Think you can cope?'

'Very funny. Is this my coffee?'

'Yes. Sit down and help yourself. I presume you still take sugar? At any rate I've added two.'

'It's still the one pleasure I cannot give up,' Rodrigo joked. Seeing the glimpse of hurt that flitted across Jenny's face, he could have bitten out his tongue. The truth was that *she* had been the hardest pleasure of all to give up. Going by the ache in his ribs and low down in his belly, she still was.

As he arranged himself at the table, a generous mug of coffee steaming invitingly before him alongside a neat round plate piled high with sandwiches fashioned out of thick-cut wholemeal bread, Rodrigo tried to smother the swift stab of longing that filled him as he stared at Jenny.

Pulling his gaze reluctantly away, he made a leisurely inventory of the homely, country-style kitchen that surrounded him. With its mismatched stand-alone oak and pine furniture, old-fashioned cooking range and long wooden shelves lined with quaint but fashionable china it was a million miles from the state-of-the-art bespoke modern interiors that his exclusive holiday resorts prided themselves on featuring. But its homespun charm was seductive and inviting all the same. In fact it reminded Rodrigo very much of the simple Andalucian farmhouse high in the Serrania de Ronda hills he had grown up in. He experienced a fierce pang of longing as the not very often explored memory unexpectedly gripped him.

'This looks very good,' he muttered, taking a swig of the burning coffee and a hungry bite of a ham and English mustard sandwich.

'If you'd arrived earlier you could have had dinner...I cooked a cottage pie, but I've put what was left of it in the freezer now. Will this snack be enough for you? I've some fruitcake you can have afterwards with your coffee, if you like.'

As she talked, Jenny brought a decorative round tin to the table and opened it. Inside nestled a clearly homemade fruitcake that smelled mouthwateringly of cloves, cinnamon and nutmeg.

Rodrigo nodded approvingly. 'I might have to take you up on that offer. You know how fond I am of homemade cake.' His well-cut lips curved in a smile. '*Is* it one of yours?'

'I made it, yes.'

'Still the little home-maker, I see, Jenny Wren.' The nickname he had settled on from the very first time they were together came out before he could halt it. The flawless alabaster skin bloomed hotly with what he guessed must be embarrassed heat. Checking his apology, he lazily watched to see what she would do next.

Outside, a flurry of stormy wind crashed against the windows, bringing with it a sleeting rush of hammering rain. Jenny's clearly affected gaze locked with his.

'Don't call me that,' she said brokenly, the volume of her voice descending almost to a whisper.

Beneath his black cashmere sweater, Rodrigo sensed tension grip his spine. 'Why not?'

'You forfeited the right when you told me our marriage was over…that's why.'

'Then I won't use it again.'

'Thank you. Besides…I told you it's the name my father always called me, and he really loved me. Eat your food, Rodrigo, you must be hungry.'

Miserable with regret, he knew that any comment he made would likely pour petrol on an already simmering fire, and automatically crammed another bite of bread and ham into his mouth. It might as well have been sawdust for all the enjoyment he received from it.

Jenny moved away across the unadorned warm brick floor to one of the many immaculately clean pine worktops that filled the room. Presenting her back to him, she started slicing up more bread from the generous-sized loaf on the breadboard, her hurried, quick movements telling him that mentioning her father had definitely made her even more upset than she was already.

'I know how much you loved him too. He raised you and your brother single-handedly after your mother died,' he remarked. 'I would have liked to have met him. I too lost my parents when I was young… remember? My father first, and then my mother.' Carrying his mug of coffee with him, Rodrigo went to join her at the counter.

Clearly startled, Jenny glanced up, her hands stilling on the knife and bread. 'Yes, I remember.'

'Their deaths spurred me on to make my own way in life…so although it was tough for a while without them I am grateful.'

'Would you—do you need that coffee topped up? The water in the kettle should still be hot,' Jenny said, anxious to move the conversation away from the dangerously personal direction it had taken.

'No, thanks. It is fine just as it is.'

'Are you sure? It's no trouble.'

Warmth spread through Rodrigo's entire being as he stared down into the lovely face before him. How he resisted the almost overwhelming urge to pull Jenny into his arms, he didn't know. Except that— as she'd told him earlier about using the pet name he had for her—he had *forfeited the right*. But the warmth that had invaded him remained, making him he realise it had been a long time since a woman had taken care of him so thoughtfully. *Not since Jenny had left, in fact.*

For the past two years he had been travelling and working abroad almost continually, and it shocked him to learn that a part of him missed that treatment. From the very first time he'd met her Rodrigo had received the impression that it was Jenny's nature to be helpful, kind and thoughtful of others. All this was coupled with an extraordinary beauty—and she had been a blessing he had hardly been able to believe had come his way.

CHAPTER TWO

'WHY don't you make yourself a drink and come and talk to me while I eat?' Rodrigo suggested, his steady dark gaze making Jenny feel as though he was putting her under a powerful microscope.

For a little while she was utterly hypnotised by his compelling examination. He was staring at her as if he honestly craved her company, and she couldn't help but feel all at sea about that. What were his motives? she wondered. It was natural to be suspicious after two years without a word. And if she was honest she was also afraid of hearing the other reasons why he'd let her go, besides the fact that he couldn't properly commit to their union because of his dedication to work. More than once at the back of her mind she'd entertained the possibility that he'd been having an affair. If that was the case then she definitely didn't want to hear about it. Rodrigo had already broken her heart, and she had no desire to have it shattered again.

'I don't have time to talk to you now,' Jenny answered nervously, tucking some corn-gold strands behind her ear. 'Besides…you've had ample time to contact me if you wanted to talk, and the mere fact that you haven't clearly illustrates what I've always known to be true: your work is much more important than any relationship. What's to be gained by digging over old ground? I picked up the pieces after our farcical marriage and made a new life, and you just returned to the one you liked best as a bachelor.'

A muscle jerked visibly in Rodrigo's high-angled cheekbone. 'What a pretty picture you paint of my conduct.'

'I'm only telling the truth. Our marriage *was* a mistake, was it not?' Her breath was so tight Jenny felt dizzy. 'I'm as much at fault as you. I had no business accepting your proposal when we'd only known each other for three short months, but I quickly learned that your work was priority number one and always would be.'

Returning to the table, Rodrigo dropped down into the chair he had vacated. Linking his hands, he lifted his dark eyes to observe Jenny. 'Why have you never spent any of the settlement I made on you?' he asked.

'Because I didn't want your damn money in the first place!' Her heart pounding fit to burst, she willed the threatening tears that were backed up behind her lids to freeze over. 'I thought I was marrying the man I loved…not entering into a lucrative business deal.'

'You have every right to the money.' Shaking his head wearily, Rodrigo surprised Jenny with a lost look that made her insides turn over. 'I let you down—made you a promise I couldn't keep. It was only fair that I compensated you for that.'

'I didn't want compensation. After the divorce I just wanted to rebuild my life and start over. I wanted to forget about you, Rodrigo.'

'And did you?'

The question hung in the air between them like a detonated grenade. Not trusting him enough to voice the truth, Jenny moved away from the pine counter and assumed a businesslike air. 'There are a few things I have to do before I turn in for the night, and I have to get on.'

'Conscientious as ever, I see. Lily has a good friend in you, Jenny.'

'She's been a good friend to me too…a real support the past two years especially.'

'She must despise me for what I did to you.' Rodrigo's mouth twisted wryly.

'On the contrary. The truth is you rarely even come into our conversation. Now, I've got to empty the rubbish and check over the house before I lock up for the night.'

'How long is Lily away?'

'She's been gone nearly three months now. She's due back in a fortnight.'

'I see. And what about the interior design consultancy that you intended to resurrect when you returned to the UK? Are you not involved with that any more?'

'I'm still running it, though business has been a bit slow throughout the summer months. That's why I was able to come here and help Lily out.'

'And how are things with your brother Tim? Are you still paying the mortgage on the family home you shared with him? I remember he had a particular talent for avoiding work and paying his own share.'

Rodrigo's question, along with his sardonic remark, made Jenny feel queasy. Of course Rodrigo had no idea what had happened when she'd returned…how sour things had turned between her and Tim—culminating in a most shocking event that she would never forget…

'Tim met somebody and moved to Scotland after I bought out his share of the house.'

'So you're still living there?'

Feeling her face throb with uncomfortable heat beneath Rodrigo's razor-sharp scrutiny, Jenny glanced away. 'I'd better go and see to those bins.'

She was still wary of further probing questions as she lifted out the recycling bag from its plastic container beneath the double butler sink that Lily had excitedly sourced from a local reclamation yard, and prayed Rodrigo would cease quizzing her.

Heading for the door opening into the utility room, she threw over her shoulder, 'Why don't you just relax and enjoy your refreshments in peace?'

'Jenny?'

Turning, she found to her astonishment that he was right behind her, his half-drunk mug of coffee left on the table. Her heart foolishly hammered at his unexpected nearness. 'What is it?'

'Let me do that for you…it sounds like a war zone out there and I don't like the idea of you coming under fire on your own.'

Even as he uttered the words a thunderous crash resounded above them, its threatening echoes rumbling like some disgruntled giant disturbed from his sleep. Once again all the lights buzzed precariously on and off, as though the whole place might be plunged into darkness at any second.

Clutching the recycling bag tightly between her fingers, Jenny shook her head. 'I'm not afraid of the storm. I'll only be gone a couple of minutes.'

Not hanging around to see if he would try to persuade her, she rushed out through the door into the utility room. Once there, she opened the back door to the part of the garden where a paved pathway led towards a sturdy iron gate, beyond which was the road. *Or where she knew there should be a road.* Switching on the night light, all she could see through the grey shroud of misty, heavily falling rain was an uprooted tree lying drunkenly across the path. The ferocious wind was tossing everything around as though it were the flimsy furniture in a child's dolls' house. Lily's beloved greenhouse was ominously shaking and shuddering. It was definitely under threat of losing its moorings as the rain viciously pelted the thin glass panes, Jenny saw. Dangerously, just a few feet away a slim-stemmed birch was being all but battered to kingdom come. If it came crashing down on top of Lily's beloved greenhouse the several almost ripened tomato plants that she'd been tending like a broody mother hen would certainly be demolished—as would every other plant and vegetable in there.

The idea of being the one who was responsible for losing them galvanised Jenny into action. Determinedly she headed for the shed at the bottom of the garden, the wind's eerie elemental power making her stumble more than once as she negotiated her way round the fallen tree that lay across the path. A while ago, whilst searching for a particular garden tool, she'd spotted what looked like a fairly robust rolled up tarpaulin inside the shed, which could now be put to good use.

The large tarpaulin clutched against her sodden chest, along with some tent pegs she'd found, Jenny shook her drenched hair from her eyes and then steeled herself to walk back to the other side of the garden where the greenhouse stood. Grimacing as another bolt of silver lightning lit up the sky, she uncurled the tarp, shaking it out as best as she could.

It didn't take long for her to realise she was fighting a losing battle. Every time she managed to get one corner straightened out the wind all but ripped it out of her now freezing hands and she had to fight to uncurl it again. The rain was like a grey blindfold over her eyes as she worked, making her curse out loud because she hadn't thought about the implications of such a storm earlier, when she'd first seen the darkening clouds appear in the sky.

'What are you trying to do?'

A voice to the side of her lifted to make itself heard above the storm. Already drenched to the skin from his dash from the back door to reach Jenny's side, Rodrigo was staring at her as though she was quite mad.

'The greenhouse!' she shouted, pointing. 'I need to secure it so it won't get flattened by the storm. I was going to throw the tarp over it and then fasten it to the ground to hold it.'

Comprehending, Rodrigo unceremoniously relieved her of the wildly blowing tarpaulin and then shoved one corner back into her hands. 'Move back and we will shake it out together,' he instructed. 'Do you have anything to secure it?'

'Yes.' She quickly stooped to retrieve the long tent pegs she'd left by her feet. 'These.' She handed them over.

'We need a hammer to bang them into the ground.' Momentarily he shifted his gaze down to her feet, as if expecting to see the necessary tool lying there.

'Oh, God.' Biting her lip, Jenny stared back at Rodrigo with an apologetic shrug. 'I forgot to bring the mallet with me. It's still in the shed.'

'I'll get it. Stay here.'

'It's at the other end of the garden. Can you see it?'

'Yes, I see it.' Before he left, Rodrigo furnished her

with a wry look. 'And do your best not to get blown away by the wind while I am gone...I am looking forward to my full English breakfast in the morning, and that's not going to happen without a cook!'

No sooner had he left than he was back again, a large wooden mallet clutched tightly in his hand, as if the storm and the fallen tree had been but mere annoying trifles that had not even vaguely threatened his mission. Taking charge with reassuring confidence, he yelled instructions to Jenny, helping them both negotiate the best way of working in the increasingly untamed weather.

By the time they had the tarp over the greenhouse roof and the sides rolled down securely over the glass walls—Rodrigo having deftly banged in the tent pegs through the loops to fasten it to the ground—Jenny felt as if she'd been packed in ice and left to freeze. *Thank God her ex had been around to help her.* That was all she could think as she took one last glance through the drowning rain at the secured tarp covering Lily's treasured greenhouse. She'd never have managed it on her own, she realised.

Gratefully dashing into the house again, she knew she must look half-drowned, with her sodden clothing and dripping hair. Next to the efficient DIY expert, who still managed to look nothing less than gorgeous even though he was also wet through, Jenny felt like something the cat had dragged in. It wasn't a picture she wanted to project to anyone...least of all the man that had broken her heart. But her hands were so chilled that she could barely even make a fist, and she had no choice but to leave the locking of the door behind them to Rodrigo too.

Dark hair was plastered to his well-shaped head, and Jenny watched an icy rivulet of water streak down his face over high-sculpted cheekbones and a clean-cut jaw that didn't have so much as a smidgeon of spare flesh detracting from its perfect symmetry. On its way, the pearl of moisture flirted briefly with a corner of his mouth, making her dangerously aware of how full and sensual his upper lip was—just like one of those Italian sculptures that art-lovers gasped at because they were so beautiful.

'Tomorrow morning I'm going to cook you the best breakfast you've ever had.' She took a nervous swallow. 'I owe you big-time for what you just did. Lily has worked so hard to grow her own vegetables, and—'

The lips that had so riveted her attention were suddenly laid over hers as gently as a butterfly wing. Shocked rigid, Jenny was nonetheless *compos mentis* enough to register the erotic warmth of the breath that came with it, as well as the burning heat hovering beguilingly beneath the rough velvet skin that had been rendered arctic cold from his rescue mission outside.

As soon as Rodrigo lifted his mouth away from hers her body throbbed with insistent hunger for a second helping of that incredibly arousing fleeting contact. The idea of having a properly passionate kiss from her one-time husband again made her feel dizzy with want…quite primitively crazy with it.

Fearing her gaze must easily reflect her torrid feelings, Jenny stepped away, her hands fiddling with the drenched ends of her shoulder-length hair, praying he wouldn't guess how violently his brief kiss had affected her. 'What was that for?' she breathed.

He shrugged, as though amused. 'Regard it as a thank-you from the absent Lily. No doubt she would be quite moved to learn that you care so much about her greenhouse that you were willing to venture outside in a violent storm to protect it.' Rodrigo smiled. 'Now…I think we both need to rid ourselves of these wet clothes before we succumb to pneumonia, don't you?'

The suggestion sounded like something X-rated articulated in that sexy Spanish voice. So much so that Jenny felt as if a fire had been lit beneath her blood. But, with his hands on his hips, Rodrigo's next words quickly brought her disturbing fantasies to an abrupt if regretful end.

'We'd better not stand here talking all night. We need to get back to our rooms, change into dry clothing and then return downstairs for a hot drink to warm us up…*sí*?'

'Good idea,' Jenny muttered, wrenching her gaze determinedly away from his. Ascending the staircase, she hurried as though being chased by some dogged pursuer up to no good. But in her heart of hearts she knew it was her own tumultuous feelings that she was really hoping to distance herself from...

In the shower, as he stood beneath the needle-sharp scalding spray, Rodrigo stared through the curtain of water, filled with disbelief at what had just happened between him and his pretty ex-wife.

Recalling the incident with more intent, he remembered that her sweet-lipped cupid's bow pink mouth had suddenly become like the most sensuous narcotic. A longing to still the tantalising little quiver he had glimpsed, to taste the heat as well as the rain-cold damp he knew he would find there, had spontaneously driven him to press his mouth against hers. What Rodrigo had not been expecting was that kissing Jenny's soft little mouth would feel so instantly essential to him the moment he made contact.

Reliving the experience made his insides dance wildly. How could he have forgotten that she could make him feel like that? His mind moved on to a far more disturbing thought. How many lovers had she taken to her bed since they had parted? She was young and beautiful, and these dark cold nights stuck out here on her own would undoubtedly get lonely. He had no right to feel so jealous and angrily affronted by the idea. Jenny was free to do as she liked. They were divorced. But if she had *not* taken a lover was it because she still thought of him?

The idea sent a burning arrow of explosive heat

straight to Rodrigo's loins and he murmured an expletive in Spanish. How long since he had had a woman? He traced the outline of a circle in the collected steam on the shower stall's glass, added a downturned mouth and scowled. *Clearly long enough for it to seriously start to bother him.*

It wasn't that there was ever a lack of opportunity. Females of all ages had taken a profound interest in him ever since he'd started to hit puberty at around thirteen. But he had done nothing about more recent opportunities because he had allowed work to gobble up his free time like an insatiable termite instead. Before he'd realised it the days and weeks in his diary had suddenly revealed that a whole year had gone by—a year during which he could practically equal a Franciscan monk for lack of sexual activity. Not to mention the complete dearth of a social life or even anything remotely related to relaxation.

He was beginning to feel a little like an auto-mated machine—going here, going there, and hardly even noticing his surroundings. It scarcely mattered whether it was some sensual eastern paradise or one of the glamorous foreign playgrounds of the rich and famous—private playgrounds to which gradually, through his single-minded dedication to his goal, Rodrigo had at last gained membership. But the successful business he'd been so focused on achieving from such a young age had gradually turned into a monster, intent on gorging every ounce of energy and life force he possessed in return for the rewards he'd once deemed so essential to his self-esteem and his life.

Frighteningly, he had experienced periods of late when his body had threatened to barely get him through the day at all. More frightening still was the fact that very little in his life—either some achieve-ment or something material—managed to give him pleasure any more. It appeared as though he was numb to the sensation. Even this new project, install-ing one of his exclusive resorts in this scenic, wild and—as research informed him—*desirable* corner of south-west England was quickly starting to lose the excitement and appeal it had initially held. But the last thing his shareholders wanted to hear was that he had lost that lucrative, moneymaking killer instinct that had helped so spectacularly to line their pockets too.

Sighing, Rodrigo stepped out of the shower onto the aquamarine tiled floor. Reaching for a volumi-nous white towel that had been left warming on the radiator, he dried himself vigorously, dressed in clean jeans and a sweatshirt, combed his fingers through his still damp hair and then turned to view his scowl-ing reflection in the steamy mirror.

He didn't like what he saw. The confirmation of his thoughts about the lack of relaxation in any form was written clear in the dullness of his eyes, in the new lines he spied round his mouth and gouged into his forehead. Even through the steam they mercilessly confronted him.

A picture came into his mind of his angelic-looking ex-wife. Would a hot night of unconstrained lust in her bed, with soft sighs, mutually hungry needs passionately met, cure him of the dullness in his eyes? Would it help him regain some of the strength and vitality that lately he sensed he had lost?

Grimacing as another wave of erotic heat seized his body, Rodrigo didn't doubt it would. But after the way he had treated her would Jenny even consider it?

As he turned to leave the room he silently acknowledged that it wasn't just the promise of a warming nighttime drink he was hoping for...

She was standing by the stove, watching over a simmering pan of milk. Somehow knowing he was there, she turned towards him and, surprisingly, gifted him with a smile. Her lovely face was scrubbed clean as a child's and her huge china-blue eyes set up such a violent longing in Rodrigo that he barely knew how to handle it. It wasn't just the natural healthy longing of a sexually aroused male at the sight of an attractive woman either. It was the totally contradictory yearning for an impossible dream that he usually dismissed as viciously as swatting an annoying fly—a dream that he had had within his grasp but had incredibly let go. But sometimes—like now—it broke through his insatiable need for success and acceptance by the world and almost throttled those desires by the throat. *Yet its tantalising promise could never be for him.* He was a pragmatist, a realist…a man a million miles away from ever putting his faith in such an impossibly unattainable idea. *No doubt his lovely ex-wife would back him up on that.*

Wearing a full-length cream dressing gown, its lapels patterned with tiny sprigged red roses, little Jenny Wren radiated the kind of innocence and purity that made Rodrigo briefly mourn for the hopefulness and joy of his early youth. *Before* he had discovered that in his ardent pursuit of success the world would extract every ounce of that hopefulness and joy and pay him back with constant growing tension and a vague unease that all was not right.

Rubbing his hand over his chest in a bid to ease the sudden clutch of discomfort that had collected there, he appreciatively registered that Jenny's golden hair had been left to dry naturally, in almost too tempting to touch blonde ringlets. Finding himself in a trance, he paused in the doorway just to gaze at her…enjoying the stirring sight she made as if paying homage to an exquisite work of art in a gallery.

'I'm making hot chocolate. Is that okay?'

'It is more than just okay. I could not think of a more perfect ending to a night like this.'

Liar, his silent inner voice mocked as he easily thought of a far more exciting and alluring alternative. But, as if to illustrate his comment, a violent blast of furious thunder overhead made the whole house feel as though the very walls were about to disintegrate into a pile of rubble.

'Sit down. I'll bring it over to you when it's ready.'

'I get the feeling that there's no one around tonight but us. Am I right in thinking I'm the only guest staying here?'

'You are. Like I said…' she whipped up the milk in the pan with a tiny whisk as if she was no stranger to the task '…we're pretty quiet at the moment. The summer holidays are long over, and it probably won't get busy again until nearly Christmas.'

'And will you still be here then, helping Lily out?'

Jenny's slender shoulders visibly stilled. 'No. I won't. I told you…she's due back in a couple of weeks and I'll be returning to London.'

'To the house you grew up in as a child.'

'Yes.'

'Yet you seem more at home here than anywhere I've seen you before.'

'What makes you say that?'

'Because this rural environment suits you… In fact, it wouldn't require a great stretch of the imagination to see you as a country girl, Jenny. Yes, I can visualise you sitting in your cosy little stone cottage each evening as the sun goes down, the tantalising smell of the day's fruitful baking lingering in the air.'

'And in this tantalising little scenario am I on my own?' The catch in her voice had Rodrigo frowning deeply.

'I don't know.' He shrugged. 'You tell *me*.' Even though his voice was calm, it felt as if an icy boulder had taken up residence inside his belly.

'You know I've always wanted a family.'

'Yes.' He shifted uncomfortably in his chair. 'I do know that.'

'But you never wanted children, did you?'

'No. I didn't.'

'Then it was just as well you decided our marriage wouldn't work, wasn't it?'

Lifting the pan off the stove, Jenny poured the steaming milk into two waiting ceramic mugs, then gave the contents a brief stir. Bringing their drinks to the table, where Rodrigo sat silently and broodingly waiting, she lowered herself into the chair opposite him. Straight away he scented the soap she'd used to wash herself with. It smelled like newly laundered linen. Once again it lit a fire in his blood that made him feel more alive and intensely aware than he had in ages.

Sighing softly, she focused her shimmering corn-flower-blue eyes on his. 'One day you might meet someone you really care for, Rodrigo, and change your mind about having children.'

'I don't think so.'

'How can you be so sure?'

'Because I know exactly what I want and what I don't want. There's no confusion about that.' His mouth set uncompromisingly.

'It must be marvellous to be so certain of things… to be so sure that you're right.'

Jenny turned her face away. When she glanced back Rodrigo couldn't pretend he didn't see the avalanche of hurt in her eyes. It all but sliced him in two, knowing he was the cause of it.

'It doesn't feel so marvellous when you put it like that,' he replied drolly.

'Then let's change the subject. Let's not talk about us—what we want or don't want—let's stick to safer topics. Your shower…was the water hot enough?'

Shrugging, Rodrigo warmed his still chilled hands round his mug of hot chocolate. 'It was fine.'

'Good.'

'You worry too much about others, Jenny.'

'I suppose I do. At least I worry that Lily's guests have everything that they need and are comfortable. It's a big responsibility, taking care of someone else's house and business, and I want to do a good job for her while I'm here.'

'Trust me…you do such a good job of taking care of your guests that you would put a top hotel to shame.'

'I suppose you'd know about that, wouldn't you?'

'I suppose I would.' Regarding her from beneath the sweeping black lashes that any female would envy, Rodrigo edged a corner of his mouth towards a smile. 'Anyway, I've always believed in acknowledging effort and good work where I see it.'

'Your staff must love you for that. As well as being paid well, everyone wants to feel valued.'

He raised an eyebrow. 'I agree. Sometimes employers can forget that.'

In his mind Rodrigo made a quick inventory of some of the people who worked for him... Were they happy? Did they consider him a good employer? Certainly his management team seemed to think so. After all, in fifteen years he had had very few complaints. From that he had to deduce that all must be well. For their loyalty and hard work he rewarded his staff with regular bonuses and luxury breaks at different foreign resorts from the ones they worked in, as well as seeing to it that they all had good pensions and private healthcare. He also knew that despite his strict adherence to high standards, he was well liked.

'So, you still enjoy your work?' Jenny enquired, dark blonde brows lifting a little.

'Yes, I do,' Rodrigo replied.

Now it was *his* turn to guard and protect his feelings. The stormy night, this warm cosy house and its unexpected pretty and familiar hostess might have lulled him into relaxing far more than he had in ages, but he was not about to confess to Jenny that lately he had fallen a little bit out of love with his chosen career.

'I suppose that was a bit of a stupid question.'

'It wasn't.'

'I mean...your work is your life, right? Of course you must still enjoy it.'

Taking a brief sip of her drink, Jenny licked the chocolate-coloured froth from her lips with the tip of her elegant pink tongue. Already feeling the disturbingly sensual effects of her alluring sweet company, Rodrigo felt the taut muscles in his belly constrict even more.

'My dad was only a plumber, but he really enjoyed his work too.' Her gaze roamed from Rodrigo's features down to his Ralph Lauren sweatshirt. 'Of course he didn't dress nearly as stylishly or expensively as you. Truth is he never made a lot of money, even though he worked hard. If he thought a customer would struggle to pay his bill he'd only charge them half the price. He wasn't a natural businessman, I'm afraid. But he was the very best father you could wish for.'

'You clearly admired and loved him very much.'

'I did. After all, what could be more important than being a good parent, and supporting, loving and adoring your children so that they don't ever doubt they mean everything to you? Being good at business is nothing in comparison to that.'

CHAPTER THREE

RODRIGO'S expression suggested an iron portcullis had slammed down over his emotions—as if everything in him, every feeling and sense, had been incontrovertibly closed and shielded against anything Jenny cared to throw at him.

She hadn't deliberately intended to make a jibe about his preference for work as opposed to having children, but she supposed it was inevitable it should come out like that. The fact was she had loved being married to him. Had prayed he would change his mind about them having a family together, and hoped his love affair with work would one day dim when it was replaced by the joys of fatherhood... But her prayers and hopes had been cruelly shattered the day he'd come home and announced their marriage was over.

It had been like listening to an icily aloof stranger, Jenny remembered with a shudder. Here in the kitchen, where the heat from the cooking range lent an air of cosiness and security as the storm rampaged outside, she wished the sense of safety and warmth she felt went beyond creature comforts. *She wished it were created by mutual love between her and Rodrigo.*

The force of her yearning made her want to weep. But she was wasting her time, dwelling on such futile things. Better that she remembered that her handsome ex-husband was just a visiting guest in the house, staying for one night only because circumstances dictated it…*not* because he'd intended them to meet and be alone together.

As soon as Lily had asked her to stand in for her for three months Jenny had vowed she'd be utterly professional and considerate at all times, and that was how she meant to proceed for the remainder of the time Rodrigo was there. She would treat him just like any other guest. She could manage that for twenty-four hours, couldn't she?

Her head swam for a moment.

'I'm going to check the house, then go to bed,' she announced, rising to her feet.

'Why do I get the distinct feeling that you're running away?' Rodrigo asked lazily.

'I'm not running away! If anyone knows how to do that it's *you*, not me.'

'You sound as though you've missed me, *querida*. Could that be the truth behind this petulant temper of yours?'

'I'm not petulant. And I haven't missed you. I'm merely getting on with my life without you and re-lieved that I'm not sitting up late every night waiting for a phone call to tell me you'll be home late or have to fly off somewhere for two weeks without me.'

'Then I've done you a favour.'

'If the idea helps you to believe what you did was right, then go ahead and think that. At any rate, I'm too tired to stand here and argue with you about it. By the way, what time do you want breakfast in the morning?'

'I'm an early riser, as you know. Seven-thirty okay with you?'

Jenny briefly met his mocking glance and forced herself not to react to it.

'Seven-thirty's fine.'

'Then I'll bid you goodnight, Jenny,' he said, taking her hint that the evening was at a close and he was most certainly going to bed alone. 'Sleep well. I hope the storm doesn't disturb you too much.'

'Goodnight,' she muttered, determinedly heading for the door.

The storm contributed to a practically sleepless night for Rodrigo. Yet he couldn't blame the turbulent display of thunder and lightning for his wakefulness entirely. The truth was he was tortured by how callously he'd ended his marriage, even though he'd genuinely believed at the time that he was doing it for the right reasons. For two years he'd held his disturbing feelings at bay, but now, being with Jenny again, they were uncomfortably surfacing.

Her words about sitting up late every night waiting

for a call to say he was coming home or flying off somewhere played over and over in his mind, driving him almost to madness. Several times he got up and walked the floor, wondering if she too was awake, like him, remembering that painful final scene between them when Rodrigo had sounded the death knell on their marriage.

At some point during the early hours, with no lessening of the fury of the storm, he crawled back into bed. A splitting headache knifing through his head, he determinedly closed his eyes, willing sleep to free him from the disturbing litany of guilt-ridden thoughts that plagued him.

When Rodrigo didn't show for breakfast at seven-thirty, Jenny put the generous plate of bacon and eggs she'd cooked in the oven, to keep them warm, then made a second fresh pot of coffee. Grimacing at the arc of furious lightning splintering overhead in the distance as she glanced out of the window, she shivered, pulling the edges of her cardigan closer over her chest to keep warm.

What was keeping Rodrigo? He was, as he'd said, an early riser.

As she continued to stare out the window through the driving rain at the reluctant dawn appearing on the horizon, she wondered if he could risk travelling anywhere in weather like this. A horrible vision of the tyres of his car skidding uncontrollably in the wet, causing the vehicle to crash violently into a tree and injure him, insinuated its way into her mind and wouldn't go away. Before she'd realised her intentions Jenny found herself apprehensively making her way upstairs. Gingerly, she knocked on Rodrigo's door.

'Rodrigo?' she called. 'Are you up yet? It's almost a quarter to eight.'

No reply. Again she rapped her knuckles against the door, her heart thudding hard under her ribs.

'Rodrigo, are you all right?'

From inside the room came a sound like a heavy book crashing to the floor. It was followed by some indecipherable low-voiced muttering. The door swung open before she had the chance to step back and Rodrigo stood there, rubbing at his eyes, his black hair more unruly than she'd ever seen it, his body encased in nothing but navy-blue silk pyjama bottoms clinging sexily low round his arrow-straight hips. The provocative sight made Jenny's mouth go dry.

Quickly pulling herself together, she folded her arms over her chest. 'Overslept, did you? That must be a first.'

'Who the hell could sleep with that din going on all night?' he retorted irritably, 'It sounded like a bombing raid!'

'It's just as wild this morning,' Jenny replied, serious-voiced, 'I don't think you should attempt to drive anywhere for a while yet…at least until things calm down.'

'Scared I might get swept off the road and end up in a ditch somewhere, *querida*?'

'That's not funny. I know male pride might convince you that you're invincible, but you'd be crazy not to listen to what I say. I've been here nearly three months now, and even in the summer the weather can get pretty scary.'

'Well, I'm neither crazy nor ignorant, and I thank you for your concern. Perhaps I'll put my meeting off for one more day and go tomorrow instead.'

Feeling a little stunned that he would even consider such an option, Jenny widened her blue eyes. 'Anyway...' she started to retreat '...your breakfast's keeping warm in the oven and I've made a fresh pot of coffee because the first one went cold. I've been up since six-thirty myself. Maybe some hot food and something to drink will revive you after your sleepless night?'

Rodrigo's suddenly amused gaze swept disturbingly up and down Jenny's figure. 'Maybe it will. Or maybe the fact that you look so wide awake and beautiful this morning will revive me even more? But that coffee sounds good too. Give me a few minutes and I'll come downstairs and join you.'

'Okay.'

Even though he'd ostensibly taken the day off, to Jenny's utmost surprise Rodrigo insisted on making himself useful, and she couldn't find it in her heart to refuse his help. At least if he was undertaking a couple of necessary DIY jobs around the house they wouldn't be at loggerheads, she reasoned. But it was disconcerting to see how impressively practical and handy he was.

Who would guess he was one of the wealthiest hoteliers in the world, much more at home in Armani tailoring and working behind a king-sized desk than getting his hands dirty in jeans and a plain black T-shirt, as he rolled up rain-damaged linoleum in the utility room and repaired some no longer properly functioning blinds in a bedroom?

The rain was still thundering against the roof when Jenny called to him upstairs to come and eat lunch. Was this relentlessly stormy weather never going to end?

Rodrigo witnessed her shiver as he came through the door into the kitchen. Immediately he frowned. 'Are you okay?'

'I'm fine. Somebody just walked over my grave, that's all.'

'What do you mean?' He was studying her with alarm.

'It's just an expression.' She smiled awkwardly. 'Nothing to worry about. Sit down—you must be starving. It's only chilli con carne on a baked potato, but it's hot and nourishing.'

'Trust me…it's very welcome'

'I never realised you had such talent for DIY.'

'I spent a lot of time with my uncle when I was young. He was a carpenter. He taught me that there is

honour in a man being able to put his hands to work.'
He pulled out a chair at the table and sat down.

'But your father wanted you to go into business?'
Jenny remembered.

'Sí he did.'

'And you never yearned to be a carpenter
instead?'

A forkful of food on its way to his lips, Rodrigo
paused to answer her. 'Maybe I did for a while...
But then I got more realistic—in terms of earning a
living, at least.'

Sitting down opposite him, Jenny made a start on
her own meal. Every now and then her gaze flicked
to the tight bronzed biceps displayed by his T-shirt
and her stomach rolled over.

They ate in an oddly companionable silence for
a while, until he glanced across at her and asked,
'Do you miss your brother since he moved to
Scotland?'

'No, I don't. You remember how difficult he could
be sometimes? Well, things got worse when I returned to the house. He felt I should just sign it over
to him completely...give him everything. He was
badly in debt because of one thing and another and
he blamed me.'

'That sounds about right—but why did he blame
you?'

'Because I'd looked out for him ever since our
parents died and he was jealous that I was getting
on well with my career and he couldn't seem to stick

at anything for long without getting into trouble. Anyway…in the end I bought him out and he moved to Scotland to live with some besotted girl he met.'

'You haven't heard from him?'

'No.' She didn't particularly *want* to hear from him either. Truth to tell, she needed more time to get over the hell he'd put her through.

His disturbing dark eyes roaming her face, Rodrigo put down his fork and stopped eating. 'You could have bought a place of your own with the settlement I made you. Then you could have just let him have the house and forgotten about him.'

Her heart racing, Jenny stared. 'I didn't want to touch a penny of that money. In fact now that we've met up again you must take it back. Do you think you're the only one who has any pride? I didn't want anything of yours after you heartlessly told me our marriage was finished. Don't you understand that? I told that solicitor of yours when he rang me about the settlement. If you wanted to cut the ties between us then we should have cut them completely! I want to make my own way in the world—just like I did before I met you.'

Could she make it any more clear how little she wanted to do with him? Each word flayed him.

Taking a long draught of the water she had poured him, Rodrigo returned the glass to the table, wiped his napkin over his lips and got up, before quietly saying. 'I should get back to what I was doing. There's still quite a bit to do. Thanks for the meal.'

She ached to say something to make him linger, but sheer hurt at the fact they were no longer together overwhelmed Jenny and she sat in silence as he walked across the floor and went out.

That evening, as they sat across the table from each other finishing their evening meal, Jenny began to realise how unwell she was feeling. Not just a tad on the warm side either. Her skin was fever-hot.

Resisting the urge to touch her hand to her head to gauge her temperature, she tugged the sides of the dressing gown she'd donned after her bath more securely over her chest. 'If this rain continues to fall we'll have to build an ark.' She smiled. 'Your carpentry skills will certainly come in handy.'

The timbre of her own voice took her aback. It sounded as if she regularly smoked cigarettes and downed whisky. *Damn!* She hoped she wasn't developing a cold. That was the *last* thing she needed when she was in a position of responsibility while her friend was away.

'Are you all right?' Rodrigo enquired, black eyes sweeping what she now knew must be her fever-bright reflection.

'I'm sorry…' Jenny mumbled. The drugging fatigue that washed over her was making her suddenly long for her bed. She pushed to her feet. 'I'm afraid I'm not feeling too good all of a sudden. I'll have to go to bed. Take your time finishing your food. There's no hurry. I mean of course it's up to you when you want to call it a day, it's just that…well…can I ask you a favour?'

'Ask away.' His dark gaze continuing to mirror concern, Rodrigo also stood up.

'Do you think you could turn off the lights for me and make sure that Cozette is in her basket before you go up to your room? She's probably hiding some- where again because of the storm. The thunder and lightning really spook her.'

'I'll do everything you ask, but will you be okay? Studying you now, I can see that you look quite fever- ish. Shall I call a doctor?'

'Heavens, no. I'm just getting a bit of a cold after being in and out of the rain, that's all. I'm sure it won't hang around long.' But all the same Jenny put her hand up to her head. Her fingers almost sizzled at the burning heat that emanated from her skin. 'I'll—I'll get a good night's sleep and I'm sure I'll be feeling back to my normal self in the morning. What time do you think you'd like your breakfast?'

'Any time that you—Jenny? Are you sure you are all right?'

'I'm fine. I just need to—' To accompany her sky- high temperature, a wave of sickness arose inside her stomach. Her sight was going worryingly hazy, and Jenny sensed the strength in her legs frighten- ingly desert her. In the next surreal moment her knees crumpled like paper and the warm bricked floor rushed towards her.

The last thing she remembered before she blacked

out was Rodrigo catching her as she fell. His arms were strong as iron bars as he swept her up close to his chest. There was a faint scent of some arrestingly exotic cologne on the air just before darkness closed in on her and she surrendered to unconsciousness with impunity…

Having found Jenny's bedroom by glimpsing some feminine clothing thrown over a chair beside a bed through a slightly ajar door on the same landing as his, Rodrigo kicked the door further open and carried her limp body across to it.

Bending a little to yank down the freshly laundered covers, he carefully lowered his charge onto smoothly ironed white sheets. As soon as he had done so she turned onto her side, clearly shivering despite the warm woollen dressing gown she wore. His heart all but missed a beat at the sound of her softly ragged breath.

Muttering a soft, 'Gracias a Dios,' that she had regained consciousness, he drew the embroidered covers carefully over her shoulders, then sat on the edge of the bed to touch the flat of his hand against her forehead. 'Maldita sea!' She was burning fiercer than the hotplate on the stove downstairs. It did not bode well. He had to act fast to help bring that temperature down, but first he had to find the telephone number for an emergency doctor.

After murmuring some consoling words in Jenny's ear, Rodrigo leapt to his feet and ran downstairs. The telephone was on the small chestnut bureau in the hallway. Picking up the receiver, he rifled through an alphabetised leather-bound address book, managing to quickly locate the number of her friend's GP. Greeted by an answer-machine message that gave him a number for emergencies only, he hissed out his frustration. Seconds later he spoke to a weary sounding male voice in person.

Explaining the reason for his call, Rodrigo was taken aback when the doctor swiftly pronounced that he couldn't possibly come out to Raven Cottage on a 'filthy night such as this'. He already had several patients to visit in the local vicinity, and unless it was a case of life or death Rodrigo would just have to take the medical advice he was about to dispense and look after Ms Renfrew himself. If her temperature did not go down within the next twenty-four hours then he should by all means ring again.

Accustomed to only having to snap his fingers and get what he needed, Rodrigo was appalled at the doctor's seemingly cavalier attitude. Wrestling the strongest urge to call the man an uncaring imbecile, he corralled his temper and quickly scribbled down the ensuing medical instructions. In any case, he had already made up his mind to ring his own personal physician in Barcelona for help should the advice he'd been given take too long to effect a change.

Back upstairs in Jenny's bedroom, he touched his hand to her forehead again. Her skin still felt hotter than a radiator with the dial turned to maximum. As

if to echo the fear that bolted through him, a deafen-
ing explosion of thunder burst violently overhead.
Refusing to believe that her condition would worsen,
Rodrigo urgently tugged down the quilt that covered
her. The warm woollen dressing gown would have to
go too.

Half lifting Jenny's limp slender form towards
him, he tried to be as quick and as deft as he could.
But his heartbeat accelerated as he observed her unnaturally rose-tinted cheeks and fluttering lashes, her
body jerking now and then as if in acute pain. Out of
the blue a partially remembered Spanish lullaby came
to him. Softly, beneath his breath, he began to sing.
*'Duerme, niña Chiquita sleep my little babe Duerme,
mi alma sleep my precious soul.'*

Lifting his hand, he smoothed some delicate
golden tendrils back from the pale fevered brow
before him. Then, with the dressing-gown cast aside,
he gently lowered Jenny back down into the bed.
The nightdress she wore underneath was a sleeveless cotton affair in white, with a chain of tiny pink
rosebuds dancing across the demure round-necked
bodice. In the innocent gown she looked like some
fairy tale princess waiting to be woken from a dream
with a kiss from a handsome enraptured hero.

Grimacing ruefully, Rodrigo levered himself to
his feet. First the lullaby he had not heard since his
grandmother had crooned it to him as a child, then
an observation that was too whimsical for words!
Ever since he had stepped over the threshold of

Raven Cottage he'd been feeling as if he was under
some kind of enchantment. But there was no time
to waste reflecting on the strangeness of his reac-
tions. Not when he had to urgently bring down that
temperature.

Hurriedly seeking out the adjoining bathroom, he
filled a decorative ceramic bowl with tepid water,
grabbed a washcloth off the towel-rail and returned
to his patient's bedside. Steeping the washcloth in the
water, he carefully squeezed it out again. Pressing
it against Jenny's forehead, then at the sides of her
neck, he murmured, 'You will be better very soon
sweetheart...I promise.'

Where did he get such confidence in his healing
powers? he wondered. Especially when the tight little
knot of anxiety that had taken up residence inside his
chest had to be a far truer indication of how he was
feeling.

'So...so hot...' she murmured, moving her head
from side to side. 'Need some...water...'

'Here.' Sliding his arm round Jenny's shoulders,
Rodrigo helped raise her head, then reached for the
carafe of water on the nightstand. Pouring some into
the matching glass, he touched the cup to her lips.
She sipped thirstily, some of the liquid escaping to
streak down her chin onto her gown.

'Please...let me lie down again.' Her sky-blue eyes
opened wide to stare up at him. 'You—you shouldn't
be doing this.'

'Why?' Rodrigo smiled, lifting an eyebrow at the

flash of lightning outside the window that for elec-
trifying moments dwarfed the dim glow of the lamp.
'What else should I be doing on a night like this? You
are ill, Jenny, and I am the only one around to take
care of you.'

'But you—you're not responsible for me any more.'
As she bit down anxiously on her quivering lower
lip her feverishly bright blue gaze was shrouded in
tears.

'Do not talk further…you will only distress yourself. Rest. That is what you must do now. It's all you
can do.'

Moving back to the bathroom, Rodrigo searched
through the mahogany cabinet for some of the regular
medication that was recommended for flu and fever.
The doctor had advised him to give some to Jenny
just as soon as he could. It would settle her and help
her have a more comfortable night. Discovering an
unopened packet near the back of the cabinet, he
scooped it up in triumph and not a little gratitude.

It wasn't the easiest task to get her to take the two
capsules he placed in her hand. She was trembling so
violently with fever. Fear slashed through Rodrigo's
insides that she might take a turn for the worst after
all. If she did then that singularly unhelpful doctor
would rue the day he had refused to come out to her,
he vowed passionately.

Biting back his apprehension and doubt, he persuaded Jenny to swallow the pills with a slurp of
water. With her eyes closed again, she turned onto

her side. A couple of minutes later she displayed all the signs of sleeping deeply.

Freeing a relieved sigh, Rodrigo scraped a hand round his stubbled jaw, studying her closely, with microscopic thoroughness. *It was no hardship to watch her...not when she resembled some slumbering angel lying there.*

Downstairs in the kitchen, a gratingly anxious *meow* greeted him. Smiling, he dropped to his haunches to gather up the softly striped ball of fur that had instantly pressed against his ankles, as though desperate for reassurance. The feline was clearly jittery about the storm, and he took a few moments to pet and make a fuss of her before popping the animal back onto the woolly plaid blanket in her basket beside the range.

Making a swift inspection of his surroundings and spying the uncovered cake of which he'd enjoyed a slice earlier, he replaced the lid on the tin so it wouldn't dry out. Satisfied that all was as it should be, he flicked off the lights and headed back upstairs. Dropping by his bedroom first, Rodrigo grabbed some paperwork relating to the meeting rearranged for the following day, dragged the satin quilt off the bed and returned to Jenny, unable to suppress the concern that had been building inside him ever since she'd fainted into his arms earlier. He was anxious to ascertain how she was doing.

He saw at once that she was still asleep, but even so he laid his cheek briefly against her chest to reassure himself that the soft rise and fall of her breathing was progressing normally. The action sent a spasm of volcanic need jackknifing through his body that almost tore his breath from his lungs. The sweetly intoxicating scent of her flesh combined with the touch of her soft breast beneath his cheekbone almost made him forget she was ill and made him long to be able to lie down beside her instead.

He glanced ruefully across at the rattan-cushioned chair he planned to spend the night in to watch over her, and his sigh was stoic. He didn't suppose he would get much sleep at all tonight, no matter *where* he slept. Not when he needed to keep his wits sharply about him to take care of Jenny. In four hours' time he would get her to take another dose of flu medication. Before that he would be sponging her down with tepid water again, to cool her temperature.

Moving across to the chair, Rodrigo stared down at the sheaf of papers in his hand. His reluctance to give the words on the page the proper attention hardly surprised him. Not when every sense and faculty he possessed was completely given over to the welfare of the lovely young woman sleeping fitfully in the bed before him. His unexpectedly dedicated commitment to his former wife left him with little desire for anything else right now.

If Jenny were well, no doubt she'd find it quite ironic. She firmly believed he had no inclination to care for anyone but himself. Many times during the brief year they'd been together she'd bemoaned the fact that he was too wrapped up in his work to spend proper time with her. Eventually Rodrigo had had to face up to the fact that he was poor husband material because it was true...he *was* married more to his work than Jenny. And that was ironic too, really, when he considered the simplicity of his mother's long-ago hope for him. Her heartfelt desire had been that her only son would find a warm, loving partner for life, father a healthy brood of children and then settle down somewhere he could be happy—preferably somewhere in Andalucia—and be content for the rest of his existence.

It was his *father* who had conditioned and programmed him from an early age to seek the lucrative rewards of a successful career in business. Benito Martinez had all but banged the idea into Rodrigo's head with a sledgehammer, giving him no choice to explore the alternatives. As a young man Benito had tried and failed to make his fortune from a house-building business. He had made some poor financial decisions and—to his shame—had lost everything. If Rodrigo achieved success in business then he, Benito, would truly be able to hold his head up in their village at last, and show them that the Martinez name meant something.

The implication had been that until such a time he would remain disappointed. And in pursuing an idea that hadn't even originated from him Rodrigo had learned that sometimes children were expected to fulfil the frustrated dreams of their parents instead of following their own...

The most disturbing images and feelings had been running through Jenny's brain. Nearly all of them involved a man who looked as if he'd stepped out of a Renaissance painting. Such endlessly dark soulful eyes he had, such glossy black hair and a heavenly shaped mouth. *His beautiful face haunted her.* His warm accented voice took her to a land of hot sun, cool Mediterranean waters and the echo of an ancient drumbeat that had been the heart of its people for centuries. Her Renaissance man also had powerful muscular arms that could carry her anywhere he wanted if Jenny allowed it, and those arms seemed to represent security and safety and something else—something essential that she'd longed for. It didn't matter right then that her fevered mind struggled to put a name to it.

A choking cough suddenly seized her. Each breathless convulsion was like a scythe slicing through her brain, it hurt so much. The arms she had dreamed of were suddenly holding her up, lifting a glass of water to her parched lips, patiently supporting and encouraging her as she gulped thirstily. Sensing her hand tremble where it circled the glass, Jenny gripped it a bit too tightly to still the tremors and accidentally tipped half the contents over her nightgown. The icy water that connected with her heated skin was akin to the touch of the coldest steel blade, and she gasped in shock.

'Oh, how stupid! What have I done?'

'It's nothing to be anxious about, *querida*, and nothing that cannot be put right in a moment. Here...I will help you remove this, then get you a towel and a clean gown.'

Before Jenny could find the strength even to protest, Rodrigo was lifting up her nightgown, bunching it into a ball, and heading off into the bathroom. Too sick to mind that he'd just seen her naked, she crossed her arms over her chest, shivering violently from a combination of fever, cold, and pure distress that she was too weak to help herself. He returned quickly, to drape a large bathtowel round her shoulders. The floral smell of lavender-scented washing detergent as well as the disturbingly sensual whiff of her ex-husband's aftershave permeated her fogged brain to cause a faint skirmish of acute awareness deep in her belly.

'Thanks.' She couldn't bring herself to raise her eyes to look at him.

'Where do you keep your clean nightgowns? In that chest of drawers over there?'

'The second one down.'

As deftly as he'd removed the wet nightgown, Rodrigo slid a fresh one down over Jenny's head and shoulders, with the same pragmatic ease. Outside the bedroom window another starburst of vivid white lightning followed by another rumble of thunder reminded her that the persistent storm had not yet exorcised its rage.

A sense of feeling safely cocooned here inside, whilst the elements caused mayhem around them, rippled beguilingly through her. It was no good feeling resentful or embarrassed about needing Rodrigo's help tonight, she concluded wearily. All she could do was surrender to the deep malaise that dragged at her limbs and made her head feel as though it was stuffed with cloth and pray and hope that when the morning came she would be over the worst and finally able to care for herself. Till then, she had no choice but to leave Rodrigo in charge.

Lowering her head resignedly against the pillows once more, Jenny shut her eyes to the surprising and hypnotic sound of his husky velvet tones softly singing what sounded very much like a lullaby in Spanish.

CHAPTER FOUR

IN THE space of a heartbeat a lovely consoling dream—a dream about a man who had a healing touch and a honeyed voice to match—turned into a nightmare of a passage in darkness, with flames licking under the only door. Jenny's pulses were wild with terror. Suddenly it was impossible to breathe. Consumed with fear that she would die there, she let words tumble from her lips incoherent and terrified as she pleaded to be rescued—pleaded for her very life.

Strong hands imprisoned her wrists and implored her to calm down in case she hurt herself. It was all right, the disembodied voice soothingly promised. Nothing was going to harm her—he would make sure of that.

As awareness of her true surroundings returned, Jenny stared frantically at the lean, high-cheek-boned face that stared back at her with rock-like steadiness in his depthless black eyes, as if whatever troubled her—however big or small—he would handle it. Her heart continued to thump crazily beneath her ribs until bit by agonising bit she recognised Rodrigo.

'It's all right,' he soothed again and the kindness mirrored back to her from his glance and his voice was like being in receipt of a warm woollen blanket on a raw winter's night. Slowly her terror started to recede. 'You were having a nightmare, baby…but you were here all the time, safe in your bed. You're burning up with fever. You're going to have to let me do what I can to help make you more comfortable.'

'A nightmare…' she mumbled through the tousled skeins of spun-gold hair that in her urgency to be free had spilled across her face.

'Don't move,' Rodrigo told her firmly. 'I'll be straight back.'

True to his word, he was, bringing with him the ceramic bowl refilled with fresh tepid water and a newly rinsed washcloth. Without words he began to apply the cloth to Jenny's face, neck and shoulders, tugging down the thin straps of her nightgown to do so, smiling directly into her eyes when her gaze dazedly fell into his.

After a while he said, 'You were screaming, "Fire!"' Neither his expression nor the tone of his voice changed as he stated this. Calmly and methodically he continued to cool her heated skin with the gently wrung-out cloth.

'I haven't had that nightmare in ages.' A violent shiver bounced up Jenny's spine like tumbleweed tossed around by strong winds. Desperately she tried to push away the cloying dark remnants of the stark cold horror that had visited her. She felt so weak and ill. But even more than the longing to be free of her sickness she craved the comfort and reassurance of someone who cared about her.

What did it say about her life that in her time of need she had to depend on the man who had left her? Was she destined to pay the price of the poor choices she had made for the rest of her days? She was so tired of being afraid, so weary of waiting for some new disaster to yet again destroy everything she'd once depended upon, leaving her with the sense that she was nervously walking a precipice that at any second she might plunge off.

'So…what makes you have such disturbing nightmares? Do you know?'

As Rodrigo touched the cool washcloth to the area just below her throat, Jenny shivered again. 'The house burned down. I—I lost everything… my parents' photos, the mementoes of mine and Tim's childhood, all our furniture and belongings… everything.'

'You were not there at the time? You didn't get hurt?'

'No. I was away when it happened, thank God. But every time I dream about it somehow I'm there in the middle of it all and I can't get out.'

'Why did you not let me know about this?' Her ex-husband's voice sounded fierce for a moment.

'We'd parted. We were no longer together and it was up to me to handle it.'

Rodrigo breathed in deeply. 'So what caused this fire?'

'The police investigation concluded it was an electrical fault.'

'That was the most incredible bad luck. But we won't talk about such distressing matters right now. It won't help. I'm going to give you some more medication to help lower your temperature and then you will sleep again.'

Letting the cloth drop back into the bowl, Rodrigo moved the items onto the nightstand then turned back to Jenny to lightly curl his hand round her delicately made wrist. Adjusting his palm, he thoughtfully stroked the pad of his thumb across the finer skin at the base of her fingers.

'And this time it will be a healing, dreamless sleep, I am certain...no more nightmares.'

'You sound so sure.'

'I *am* sure.'

'Why?'

'Because my intuition tells me so.'

'You believe in that?'

'I do.'

After swallowing down the two capsules that Rodrigo gave her with a few sips of water, Jenny smiled shakily. 'You should have been a doctor.'

'What? And deprive the hotel business of my incredible flair and superb know-how?'

'You'd be superb at whatever career you chose, Rodrigo. You would have made the best carpenter too.'

Unable to ignore the weariness that was like a powerful warm wave taking her under, Jenny slid back down into the bed, her eyelids closing even before her head touched the pillow. She'd happily accept the idea of a dreamless sleep, she silently admitted. But she'd equally welcome another dream of a man with sable eyes deep enough to swim in and a gentle sure touch that was far more healing than any medicine...

For a long time after Jenny had returned to the land of sleep Rodrigo sat in the rattan chair, listening to the rain lash furiously against the windows, soberly mulling over what she'd told him about her family home burning down and losing everything.

He had been drifting off himself when her anguished cry had rent the air and sent him bolting out of his seat as if an explosion had just ripped through the room. But even though his heartbeat had thundered in alarm, he'd still had the presence of mind to stay calm, so that when she emerged more fully from whatever nighttime horrors had visited her he could reassure her that it was only a dream. Those incandescent blue eyes of hers definitely didn't lack courage, but he'd sensed early on in their acquaintance that there was some fragility in her make-up too.

It had made it all the harder for him to end a

marriage that should never have happened in the first place. But Rodrigo had been so head over heels in love with Jenny from the instant he'd seen her chatting to a friend, one of the receptionists at the hotel he'd been staying at in London, that for a while he hadn't been thinking straight.

Now, after witnessing the distress caused by her nightmare, Rodrigo willingly resigned himself to the fact that he would be getting no sleep for the rest of the night. How could he risk even dozing if that fever of hers got worse? It was vital to stay alert in case he had to make an emergency dash in his car to the nearest hospital. But even the idea of negotiating a safe path through this hostile storm in the pitch-dark, in an area he wasn't even familiar with, keeping one eye on his possibly dangerously ill passenger as he drove, filled him with dread. Yet there was no question that he would do what had to be done and deliver Jenny safely into the competent medical hands she deserved...

Grimly firming his mouth, he beat his fingers in a soft, restless tattoo on the arms of his chair. It was best not to concentrate on the worst-case scenario, he decided. If Jenny woke suddenly he would not want her to sense that he was rattled by the situation in any way.

Needing a distraction, he reached for the sheaf of papers he had brought from his room, resolving to concentrate.

Two hours later the thunder and lightning was at

last a spent force, the storm having subsided to the ghostly sound of the wind rushing pell-mell through the trees and faintly rattling the windows. Judging by the hushed rhythmic breaths that had softly accompanied the reading of his documents Jenny was still sleeping peacefully, and a welcome atmosphere of calm had descended on the room.

His eyes feeling as if he'd rinsed them out with gravel, Rodrigo laid down his papers and stood up. Yawning and stretching, he moved barefoot to Jenny's bedside. Glancing down at her angelic profile—at the curling dark blonde lashes brushing the tip of her velvet cheekbone, the slim, elegant nose and lips as serene as those of the blessed Madonna herself—he felt a rush of forceful commanding need rock him to his soul.

After helping her change her gown during the night and seeing her naked once again it was hard to get the arresting image of her bewitching perfection to leave his mind. *She was so lovely that Rodrigo had to force away the idea of her being with someone else.* It made him feel jealous and suddenly possessive. If he had a second chance with her then he would definitely *not* spend all his time at work. Even *he* must learn from the lessons of the past.

Suddenly realizing the road his hypnotized thoughts were taking him down, Rodrigo shook his head. For heaven's sake, was he going mad? His marriage to Jenny was finished—over. He'd made his choice and he was destined to live by it. Dedication and hard work had helped him become the owner and head of one of the most successful luxury spa hotel empires in the world, and he wasn't about to ease off the gas for anything—least of all a precarious rekindling of a relationship that he'd really known from the first could never work. The only real solace and satisfaction to be had in life was in his work. No woman, no matter how soft, feminine and lovely, could bring him more happiness and fulfilment than that. He might indulge his need for sex and companionship from time to time, but that was all.

Moving away from where Jenny lay peacefully sleeping, in case he was tempted to meander into the realms of such pointless fantasy again, he rubbed his palm round his unshaven jaw with a scowl. Reaching the window, he swept the curtain aside to see the faint pink and gold light of dawn edging the horizon. Hovering over the smooth glass of the sea, it was a sublime sight. *A sight surely worth missing out on a night's sleep for...* It didn't happen very often that he did that. The strict routine he adhered to didn't factor in long, soulful glances at charming scenery.

'Rodrigo?'

'*Sí?*'

He spun round with a jolt to find Jenny throwing back the covers and lifting her legs out of the bed.

'What time is it?'

'Just after seven a.m. Where do you think you're going?'

Reaching her side, Rodrigo frowned deeply. To

MAGGIE COX 75

his surprise she kept her head bowed and he sensed she was embarrassed.

'I—I need the bathroom.'

'Let me help you.'

'I can manage.'

But even as she strove to rise to her feet he saw that she was trembling like some fragile birch leaf in the wind. It was clear she was still feverish, and far from recovered.

'I disagree.' His tone strongly disapproving, Rodrigo had no hesitation in scooping her up into his arms and marching into the bathroom. Through the paper-thin cotton of her nightgown her body heat all but scorched him. There was no way on earth that she'd be fit enough to run her friend's guesethouse for a good few days yet. He also knew he wouldn't or *couldn't* leave her stranded. His scheduled business meeting would just have to be postponed again. No doubt his contractors would be relieved to have the extra time to get things ready for the boss's inspection.

Switching on the light, Rodrigo carefully stood Jenny down in the middle of the floor. And, because he couldn't resist, he gently moved a few tousled strands of corn-gold silk back from her face. 'I will be waiting right outside the door to help you back to bed,' he told her. The unsullied crystal of her huge blue eyes reminded him of an Andalucian mountain lake, caressed by sunlight. His stomach rolled over at the sight.

'Okay…'

When she emerged from the room a few minutes later Rodrigo once again swept her up into his arms to carry her back to bed. As she settled back under the covers Jenny's expression was forlorn. 'I'm so embarrassed that I've let you do all this for me that I almost don't know what to say to you.'

'Were you well last night?'

'No, but—'

'Are you feeling any better today?'

'No… But I still—'

'Is there someone—some friend, family member or even a neighbour I can ring—who will come and take care of you for the next few days?'

Rodrigo didn't miss the flash of despair in her eyes. 'Not that I can think of…no…'

'Then there is nothing else for you to do but go back to sleep. I am here, and will remain so until such time as you are able to get back on your feet and go about your business as normal. If anyone rings to make a reservation then I'll simply tell them we are closed until you are better.'

'But what about your work? You came down here for a meeting, didn't you?'

'It is easy enough to delay for another day or two.'

'You would do that for me?'

'I know you find that hard to believe but, yes, Jenny…I *would*.'

'Even so, I can't let you, Rodrigo.'

'You have no say in the matter. It's my own decision. No one is forcing me to do anything I don't want to do—least of all you.'

'I feel so useless.' Her pretty mouth struggling with emotion, she looked as if she might cry.

Still feeling appalled that there was no one Jenny could ask to help but him—his own past neglect of her not withstanding—Rodrigo gave her a gentle shove so that her spun-gold head fell back onto the creamy white pillows.

'Since I have already complimented you on your ability to make guests feel more than at home here, and have seen how dedicated you are to running things for Lily in her absence, that's clearly not true. Go back to sleep. When you wake I'll make you a cup of tea, if that's your preference. But I warn you that my tea-making skills would hardly earn me a job working here.'

Chuckling, he reached out to lay his palm flat against Jenny's forehead. She was still unnaturally warm, but thankfully not as dangerously hot as last night. Cautiously, he prayed that meant her fever had broken and she was over the worst.

'You're a long way from recovered, *querida*, but hopefully you are on the mend. Right now I need a shower and a shave—then I'll see what has to be done downstairs. Do as I say and get some more rest... I'll return in a while to make sure everything is okay.'

Settling back against the bank of pillows she'd just about mustered the strength to arrange behind her,

Jenny swept her gaze round the sunlit bedroom with frustrated resignation and felt a little jab of fear piercing her. It was perfectly true that she felt weaker than a newborn foal, and twice as vulnerable, but to have allowed Rodrigo, her work-obsessed ex-husband, to postpone his business meeting to help take care of her... Well, it hadn't featured in even her *wildest* dreams. *And why had she trusted him so easily when his past record of considering her needs was so abysmal?* It was inexplicable.

She'd had similar issues with Tim. Jenny knew her brother wasn't the type of man who could take care of anything much. He certainly wouldn't have been able to even look after their home if she should have fallen ill. In truth, he would have simply gone out and left her. His attitude to any sort of responsibility was casual, to say the least. When she'd returned to live in her old home after she and Rodrigo had split up, the beautiful Victorian semi she'd grown up in had been an absolute *tip*. It had taken several weeks of diligent home-making application on Jenny's part to restore it to anywhere near its former beauty and comfort.

Then, after months of growing suspicion of her brother's irresponsible behaviour, she'd discovered the real reason he was inclined to let things slide— and that included work. It was because he despised any demands that came between him and his increasing dependence on drugs.

A flutter of pain tightened her chest. *Dark times...*

Not the kind of thing Jenny wanted to recall when she was feeling so poorly.

In stark contrast, the vibrant and charismatic Rodrigo had taken on the mantle of carer so gallantly and effortlessly that she was already half bewitched by him all over again. *Dangerous.* Her temperature had soared even higher when he'd swept her up into his arms to take her to the bathroom and back to bed when she came out. There was no disputing the man's strength, or the beguiling warmth of his body at close quarters, or the fine and expensive way he smelled. But the situation couldn't continue for much longer, Jenny vowed. Somehow she had to get better quickly to resume her stewardship of Lily's guesthouse. It was kind of Rodrigo to say he would tell people they were closed until she was recovered, but it was her friend's precious income she was denying if she allowed that.

'How are you feeling?'

The man himself stood in the doorway, carrying a tray with a cup of tea on it. The sight of him had the same effect as a shot of dizzying adrenaline in the arm. He was wearing a fitted coal-black T-shirt and faded light blue denims that hugged his muscular thighs like a glove. The deceptively ordinary clothing must *love* being so close to his smooth bronzed skin, Jenny thought wildly, because the things they did for that mouthwateringly fit body surely shouldn't be allowed in a defenceless woman's bedroom.

Flustered, she sat up a bit straighter against her

pillows. 'I thought about lying to you and telling you that I felt much better, but if I got up and fell flat on my face I realised you'd pretty soon get the picture that perhaps I should have made a will…just in case.'

'At least you've got your sense of humour back. That's got to be a good sign. And you're not going to die…not on *my* watch.'

Moving towards the bed, Rodrigo deposited her cup of tea on the nightstand.

'Room service as well?' Jenny quipped, wishing it wasn't so hard to breathe whenever he came near. 'Did you master that when you were starting out in the hotel business too?'

CHAPTER FIVE

'IF YOU want to learn how a business works from the ground up then you have to familiarise yourself with everything.'

'I agree. When I first started doing interior design I found there were so many dimensions to it that I hadn't realised. It made the work even more interesting, though.'

'And how's business these days?' Rodrigo asked.

'It's been a bit up and down, which is why I could come here and help Lily out. But I've got a couple of good commissions coming up.'

Her plump lower lip was receiving some unfair treatment from her teeth as she chewed on it, he observed.

'Anyway…from what you say about the way you approach things it's obvious that you've become a success because you're so…thorough.'

The corners of his mouth edged into a sardonic smile. 'I am, as you say thorough. That applies to whatever I might be engaged in, if you recall.'

Jenny lapsed into a self-conscious and pink-cheeked silence. Had the same stimulating scenario gone through *her* mind as had just flashed through his? *Rodrigo certainly hoped so.*

'Thanks for the tea. You've made it exactly the way I like it.'

'Muchas gracias, señorita.' He made a mock bow. 'I aim to please. Here.' Carefully he passed her the cup and saucer, noting immediately that her hands shook a little as she accepted it. 'And after you drink it you are to stay put for the rest of the day. I'll see to everything else that needs to be done.'

'I'll have to pay you for your help, Rodrigo.'

'What?'

'It's only right. If you're working for me I'll have to pay you…especially as I'm delaying your return to your own job.'

'That's crazy talk. You need do no such thing.' A spasm of anger shot through him that she would think for even a second that he expected to be paid for helping take care of her when she was ill. 'Now that the rain's stopped I'm going into the garden to check on the greenhouse. I'll remove the tarpaulin we put up the other night and look over any damage that the storm might have caused. For lunch I'll make us a simple soup—my cooking skills do actually exceed my tea-making ones, though I confess I didn't demonstrate them when we were together. You were clearly a bit rundown for this fever to have occurred and no doubt your immune system needs building up again with good food.'

'Right now I couldn't contemplate eating any- thing—not when my sense of taste is probably non- existent.' Taking the tiniest sip of the hot tea he'd made, Jenny passed him back the delicate blue and white cup with its matching saucer almost immedi- ately. 'I don't mean to sound ungrateful, but I feel so stupidly weak that I—' Touching her hand to her head, she grimaced.

'Does something hurt?' Rodrigo demanded, examining her flushed pretty face with renewed concern.

'My head feels like a re-enactment of the Battle of Waterloo is going on inside it,' she answered. 'I really need to shut my eyes again. Do you mind?'

'Of course not... It's clear that you are nowhere near recovered.' After returning her cup and saucer to the nightstand, when next Rodrigo looked she'd slid back down into the bed and buried herself beneath the plump feather duvet like a small animal going into hibernation.

'Rest, then, *querida*,' he said with a smile, and although he would have been quite happy to stand and gaze at her for a while longer, he wrestled the desire to the ground and headed back downstairs.

During the following three days it honestly went through Jenny's mind more than once that if she slipped away into the afterlife one fever-racked night it might be a blessing. Never before had her constitution been under such miserable threat. But she held onto the vehement assurance that Rodrigo had given her— 'You're not going to die...not on *my* watch.'

Had she ever slept this much in the whole of her twenty-seven years? Her dad had told her once that even as an infant she had only slept six hours out of every twenty-four. *Not much rest to be had then for her long-suffering parents.*

But during those memorable three days while she was ill Jenny heard Rodrigo moving reassuringly round the house, doing this and that, and at one point forced opened her heavy lids to see a smart-suited stranger urging her to 'just relax' whilst he placed a cold thermometer under her arm to take her temperature. Whatever the doctor concluded it had caused Rodrigo to move into her bedroom permanently, it seemed—because whenever Jenny did manage to open her eyes he was there in the rattan chair next to her bed, either scribbling away on a notepad with his pen or tapping away at the keys on his laptop. A couple of times she registered him speaking on the phone too...once in mellifluous Spanish.

But, as much as his continued presence reassured her, Jenny had mixed emotions about it. Her tired brain could hardly credit why he would stay with her for so long and not simply leave... It was nothing like his old behaviour, when work had always come first.

On the fourth day of her illness she woke up

feeling less likely to die and longing for a bath. Her teeth were also in dire need of the brushing of a lifetime, because frankly her mouth tasted as though some small creature had crept inside and died in it. It was after eight in the morning, and the rattan chair beside her was empty of her handsome dark-haired guard. With a little jolt of unease in her stomach at the fresh realisation of just how much she had been relying on Rodrigo she swung her legs over the side of the bed and stood up.

Wrong move, Jenny... The room spun alarmingly, as though she'd just stepped off a manically twirling carousel

'What are you doing?'

'I need a bath. If I don't have one soon you'll have to report me to the health and safety department.'

Moving away from the doorway, his face unsmiling, Rodrigo walked right up to her. Recently showered and shaved, and wearing a fresh white T-shirt and black corded jeans, the man smelled *gorgeous*. It made Jenny all the more flustered and aware of her own less than scented condition after lying ill in bed for three days.

'Are you up to having a bath, *querida*? Perhaps I could bring a basin of warm water and you could have a bed-bath instead?'

'With you playing nurse?' Her eyebrows flew up to her scalp. 'I don't think so!'

'This is hardly the time for false modesty, Jenny Wren. Besides...' a teasing spark of heat ignited in his soulful dark eyes '…I've seen you naked, remember? And not just when I helped you change into a fresh nightgown.'

She'd been praying she'd dreamt that. Learning that wasn't the case, she felt her heart skip an embarrassed beat. 'It's hardly gentlemanly of you to remind me about that.'

He chuckled—a husky, compelling sound that made her legs feel weaker than water. 'Sometimes I am a gentleman and others *not*. I don't have to leave it to your imagination to wonder about the times I am not…do I?'

Clutching the front of her nightgown a little desperately, Jenny tipped up her chin. 'I have to have a bath. In fact I insist. Just leave me alone for a while, would you? I'm quite capable of sorting it out for myself.'

But he'd already stalked into the bathroom and turned on the taps. Stepping back into the bedroom, he dropped his hands to his hips, grinning with a distinct air of amused defiance at her disbelieving look. 'Which bubble bath shall I pour in? You have several.'

'I—I…' Flustered, she bit heavily down on her lip again. It might appear ridiculous to Rodrigo to quibble about such an innocuous thing, but somehow pouring in her bath fragrance seemed like the ultimate in intimate acts when she was already feeling disconcertingly fragile. 'I'll do that.'

Moving into the already steam-filled bathroom on

legs that felt like cotton-wool, Jenny shouldn't have been a bit surprised to find Rodrigo right behind her, but she was.

'This is no time to be petulant,' he told her, stern-voiced. He stepped in front of her, his black eyes roving her face as if he would know the secrets of her very soul. 'Which fragrance shall I use? If you won't tell me then I will put in the rose...especially since you reminded me of one from the moment I saw you in the reception area of the Savoy Hotel.'

Stoically resisting a huge urge to cry, Jenny scanned the array of prettily shaped bottles on the shelf above the bath and sniffed. 'That's the most ridiculous thing I've ever heard.'

Rodrigo took hold of her elbows and impelled her towards him, so that she had no choice but to make him the sole focus of her attention. 'You didn't always throw my compliments back in my face, Jenny... No,' he added lazily, 'sometimes they could make you blush, and other times make you extremely affectionate as I recall.'

Now, as heat cascaded through her like a rampaging river, Jenny's legs really *did* feel as if they might not hold her up for very much longer. There was a heaviness and a heat between her thighs she couldn't deny.

'That was when I trusted and loved you,' she burst out irritably, pulling free of Rodrigo's loose hold on her—suddenly terrified of the need that made her want to surrender to his arms and give him everything. 'And I don't any more. Now I'm much more careful about who I give my affection to.'

'Is that your way of telling me you've found some-one else?'

'Are you joking?' she answered scathingly. 'After the way my brother behaved as well, I don't think I'll ever trust another man again.'

'Not now, perhaps... But when enough time has passed you might learn that not all men are so de-spicable.' Tenderly Rodrigo smoothed back her hair, standing his ground as Jenny's body stiffened with tension

'If I ever make the mistake of trusting a man again, then I deserve everything I get!'

'Yet you *did* trust me again.' His tone was gentle but firm. 'You trusted me to take care of you while you were ill.'

'I didn't have much choice, did I?'

'Do you want to vent your anger at me Jenny? Is that it?'

'All I want is my bath,' she said weakly. Frighteningly, she sensed that the full flood of grief and pain over what had happened between them hov-ered dangerously close now that she'd opened the lid on it again. It must be because she was sick she reasoned. Usually she managed to contain her hurt and rage much better.

'Then that's exactly what you shall have.' Reaching up to the shelf for the crystal bottle labelled 'English Rose,' Rodrigo gave her an unperturbed smile. After liberally applying it to the splashing hot water, he returned the bottle to the shelf. 'I'll leave you to get into the tub by yourself, but if you need me I'll be just outside the door,' he told her.

'Thanks,' she murmured. And as soon as the closed door was a barrier between them she dropped down onto the loo seat and allowed herself to listen to the sound of her heart breaking again...

That was when I trusted and loved you, she'd said. He could drive himself mad with regret and pain because she'd never say she loved and trusted him again. And it wasn't easy for Rodrigo to leave Jenny to cry. He'd sensed the hurt she normally held in strict check had just catapulted to the surface and spilled over. Every heaving sob was like a knife slicing through his heart, and it disturbed him to discover that he could be so affected by this woman's tears.

Why had it not been that way before? The more she had cried, the more he had been furious with what he saw as typically female behaviour employed to manipulate his emotions. He sat in the rattan chair and dropped his head in his hands. Listening to Jenny's distress was nothing less than pure torture.

A few moments later, the sound of her crying ceased. Resisting the strongest urge to knock on the door and ask if she felt better, he heard the relieved groan she released as she settled herself back into the hot water. About five minutes later, lost in his own thoughts, Rodrigo jolted when he heard her call out his name. He was at the door in a second.

'What is it? Are you okay?'

'Can you—can you come in?'

Surprised, he didn't hesitate. Such a picture she made, lying there amidst the fragrant pink bubbles, her big blue eyes staring back at him like a crestfallen child's, that Rodrigo's heart slammed hard against his ribs.

'Do you want me to scrub your back?' he joked, although the idea of sliding his hands over that gleaming wet satin skin was definitely no cause for amusement. Even as he stood looking down at her his body throbbed with equal measures of pleasure and pain.

'Could you help me wash my hair?' Jenny asked softly, her expression clearly nervous in case he should refuse.

'Of course… Where is your shampoo?'

'Here.' She handed him a tube-shaped bottle.

Dropping to his knees behind her, Rodrigo breathed her in, stealing a vital couple of moments to contain the lava-flow of desire that rocked through him and stay clear-headed enough to do the job in hand. But every sense he had was already saturated with her essence, even before he touched her.

Applying some shampoo to her already dampened hair, he could hardly attest to breathing as he began to move his palms slowly over her scalp. Nobody had ever told him that washing a woman's hair could be so immensely satisfying and erotic. Over one satiny-smooth shoulder he glimpsed the delicate swell of her breast, disappearing provocatively down into a sea of pink foam.

'Rodrigo?'

'Yes?' His voice sounded as if it scraped over gravel, he was so aroused.

'I'm sorry I acted like such an idiot just now. Perhaps we can call a truce?'

'I'm not at war with you, Jenny. I never was.'

'What do you mean?'

Jenny turned her head to glance at him, and he painfully observed the tiny collection of moisture bubbles clinging to the delicate furrow above her top lip. He yearned to lick away every one.

'I've never thought of you as my enemy…that's all.'

'So you want us to be friends? Is that what you're saying?'

'*Dios!* I know you are ill, but I don't want you to delude yourself that it's friendship I'm interested in! Pass me that jug so I can rinse your hair, would you?' He clicked his fingers, scarcely able to contain his impatience and—it had to be admitted—his *annoyance*. Suddenly he was in no mood for playing games. Not when it was all but killing him to wash her hair.

'Are you mad at me for asking you to do this?' When Rodrigo had finished rinsing, Jenny hurriedly scraped her fingers through her damp shoulder-length locks to move them out of her face, her gaze anxiously tracking him as he stood up and moved round the tub to survey her.

'No. I'm not mad at you at all. But don't fool yourself that all I want to do is take care of you while you're ill. Trust me...I'm not as selfless or gallant as you may imagine. Neither am I made of stone.'

'Oh.'

'Is that all you can say?'

'Rodrigo, I didn't ask you to stay and take care of me. Are you saying that I should sleep with you as some kind of thank-you?'

'Dios!'

His handsome face looked so thunderous that Jenny shrank back as far as she could in the tub, her heart beating hard.

'That you even *dare* make such a crass remark is beyond belief. Admitting that I desire you does not mean I'm suggesting you give me your body for services rendered! I know perfectly well that you're not immune or unaware of the attraction flaring between us again. I was merely being honest about my intention.'

'And that is?'

He curled his lip in a sardonic smile, then folded his arms across his chest. His action drew Jenny's heated gaze to the ripple of toned hard muscle in his bronzed biceps and taut torso, and she felt the hot sting of arousal burning in the tips of her breasts.

'I am definitely going to make love to you very

soon, Jenny,' he drawled. 'I will, of course, wait until you are fully recovered, but make no mistake that it will happen. Now... Do you need my help getting out of that tub?'

'No!' she answered quickly, disconcerted to see him nod with a little mocking smile.

'Okay, then. If you think you can manage on your own then I'll go downstairs and prepare some breakfast for us. You are hungry this morning, yes?'

Hungry? Suddenly the word had all kinds of dangerous connotations for Jenny.

CHAPTER SIX

CURLED up on the living room couch with a cosy woollen blanket, Jenny watched Rodrigo rise from where he'd been stoking the burning logs in the woodstove, then smooth his long artistic hands down his jeans. Although she was still feeling frustratingly tired and achy, it was impossible not to notice how strong, well made and fit he was. He might work in the hotel trade on the business side of things, but he wasn't a man who shied away from hard physical work either.

Earlier, she'd glanced out of the kitchen window to see just how hard he'd been working in the storm-tossed garden. It looked as if it had been given a serious face-lift. Even the fallen tree had been moved to lie safely against the fence, and without its temporary tarpaulin Lily's beloved greenhouse appeared intact and sturdy as ever.

'You'll be wanting to head off soon, now that I'm feeling better.' Suddenly, the thoughts that had been buzzing round inside Jenny's head were out in the open.

Remaining quiet, Rodrigo strode across to lay his palm against her forehead. A hot current of awareness hummed right down to the very edges of her toes.

'You are still a little warm.' He frowned, his ebony gaze sweeping over her like an arresting searchlight.

'Yes, but I really am feeling so much better.'

'But hardly well enough to get back to work and run Lily's business efficiently. Today is Friday…I'll stay until Monday at least, to make sure you are well on your way back to being fighting fit before I go.'

'You don't have to.'

In answer to that comment, he merely raised an eyebrow.

'By the way, I've been meaning to ask you… Have we had any enquiries about bookings over the last few days?'

'*Sí*…we have.'

'And?' Jenny's hands twisted anxiously in the folds of the woollen blanket.

'And I made the required reservations, of course. They were both for the end of the month, when your friend returns from Australia. A married couple from Jersey and a single woman from Edinburgh. All the details are in the reservations book.'

'She'll be pleased about that. Thanks for seeing to things. You've been working hard in the garden too, I noticed. I can't let you do all this for nothing.'

'We have already put that subject to bed, have we not?'

'Okay...I'll drop it. But as soon as I feel able I'll cook you something nice.'

Cozette chose that particular moment to stroll into the room and make a beeline for Jenny's lap.

She grinned in delight as she stroked her hand over the deliciously soft striped fur. 'Cozette, my angel! How have you been, baby? Have you missed me?' The cat rubbed its face against Jenny's arm, then settled into the blanket against her middle to purr contentedly.

'Little traitor.' Rodrigo grinned, dropping easily down to his haunches to fondly pet the animal.

'A traitor... Why?'

'Because since you've been ill she's behaved like I am the sun, moon and stars—playing up to me, wanting me to pamper and pet her whenever she gets the chance...just as if she lives for nobody's attention but mine. Now she's with you I see that she was merely toying with my affections, like the typically mercenary little female she is!'

'All females aren't mercenary, Rodrigo.' Imbuing her tone with a teacher-like scold, Jenny bravely met his mocking glance. Almost instantly the humour in his eyes vanished, leaving her with the strangest sensation that she was falling through space—plummeting at frightening speed—with no sense or idea of when or *if* she would land safely on earth again. A gasp caught and died in her throat as he reached for her hand to place it firmly against his rough-velvet cheek.

'I find myself intensely jealous of the attention that you're paying Cozette, *querida*…I'm wondering if you have any left to spare for me.' Moving her palm to his lips, he pressed a warm kiss into the centre.

'I expect you've been missing the routine and demands of your work.' Keeping her voice deliberately light, so that he wouldn't see how affected she was, Jenny retrieved her hand to lay it over Cozette again. She prayed Rodrigo wouldn't see that it was trembling. 'Your friends are probably missing you too. I feel slightly guilty that I've monopolised your time because of this stupid illness.'

'So you expect never to get ill? You are infallible?'

'I didn't mean that. All I meant was that it was inconvenient.'

'You know my lifestyle. I travel too much to be concerned with friends.'

Shrugging, Rodrigo rose to his feet, briefly rubbing his hands together.

'You don't always have to isolate yourself from people, Rodrigo.'

'I am perfectly happy with the way things are.'

'Really?' It hurt Jenny to hear that.

'I find it works better for me if I keep a little distance.'

'But still…don't you get a bit lonely, doing all that travelling and never really being close to anyone?'

'My work is my life. You of all people know that.

Now, I've got some phone calls to make that have been backing up. Are you okay by yourself for a while?'

'Yes, I'm fine.' Her heart thudding heavily, because Rodrigo suddenly seemed to be clearly illustrating his preference for a little distance, Jenny sighed.

'At least you have Cozette for company, no?'

'I told you—I'm fine. I don't need a babysitter… Just go and make your phone calls and forget about me.'

'I'll make my phone calls…but I won't forget about you, Jenny Wren.'

Because he'd taken the wind out of her sails, Jenny glared at him. 'Just go!'

'Okay, okay, I'm going.' Having the audacity to chuckle at her petulant tone, he held up his hands in a gesture of surrender and backed slowly out of the room.

As soon as he was gone, Jenny was appalled to find hot tears boiling up behind her eyes. Suddenly the prospect of him leaving made her stomach lurch with sadness. What was the matter with her, for good-ness' sake? She was over him, wasn't she? What on earth was she doing, attaching herself to the idea that somewhere deep inside he perhaps still held a torch for her? They'd parted a long time ago now. Why couldn't she just accept that and get on with her life as she'd been doing before he'd shown up?

Lifting her hand up to her face, she stared at the

spot that his lips had so spine-tinglingly caressed. It throbbed like a brand. Did he still not need anyone at all...ever?

In the afternoon, after the light lunch he'd prepared for them both, Rodrigo absented himself again, leaving Jenny with a stack of DVDs to choose from to keep her entertained. It appeared she was in no mood for conversation.

Seeing definite signs of her recovery, even though her complexion was still marble-pale, he took the opportunity to return to his room to work. Yet from time to time, as he studied his paperwork and made his phone calls, he couldn't help remembering how they'd been captured by each other's gazes just before he'd kissed her palm. It caused a flutter of mayhem in his stomach to recall it. Irritable, but not wanting to explore why, he diverted his attention to his most pressing phone call.

It had been just as he'd thought at the site in Penzance—the building schedule had indeed fallen behind, and even more so with all the rain. Although Rodrigo had had to delay the meeting because of Jenny, he now wanted to get to the root of the hold-up. There were several things he wanted the manager to keep him up to speed with, in fact, which meant that the afternoon flew by in a long, detailed discussion until Rodrigo had thoroughly satisfied himself that all was now proceeding as it should be.

Rising from behind the antique desk in his room,

he rolled his shoulders to unlock the cramps in his muscles. Sighing, he strolled across to the window. In the far distance the sun-kissed silver Atlantic lapped the sand-covered shore, the white foam rolling in and out again as it had done since time immemorial but no-less mesmerising. Narrowing his gaze, he observed the seagulls cutting cleanly across the winter blue sky that would soon turn to dusk, dipping gracefully every now and then into the ocean in avid search of their supper. An urgent need suddenly arose inside him to breathe in some of that wild sea air.

Jenny was dozing on the couch when he looked in on her and so, deciding to follow his impulse, Rodrigo drove down to the beach.

She was definitely over the worst, he assured himself, so he could risk leaving her to sleep for a while. He tucked his rich burgundy cashmere scarf deep into the neckline of his leather jacket and strode across the sand, wincing but enjoying the bracing air. On Monday, when he left this place, his usual routine would be quickly reinstated, he reflected. Jenny would no longer need his help, so work would once again take precedence.

A sharp twist low down in his belly protested at the idea with a painful jolt. It was merely frustration, Rodrigo thought impatiently—frustration at not being able to satisfy his lustful desire for his pretty ex-wife. He knew he'd sworn that he would make love to her soon, but the more he thought about it, the more he guessed that wouldn't be wise. Jenny still had dreams in her eyes, he realized, and if he got involved with her even briefly and then left again it would no doubt reinforce her angry belief that cruelty was indeed inherent in his character.

No... He just had to put any further thoughts of bedding her right out of his mind. Instead, as soon as his business meeting was over, he would return to London where he could hook up with a Spanish actress he knew. He occasionally took her to dinner— and more often than not to bed. She was a real Latin firecracker, and knew all kinds of stimulating ways to entertain and relax a hard-working man.

But the thought of the red-lipped fiery *señorita* left Rodrigo cold when he compared her charms to the warm and beguiling Jenny.

Biting back a ripe curse, he saluted an old man who was walking a terrier, then—with his head down against the strong gusting wind—retraced his steps back to the car.

'Where did you go?'

'I took a walk on the beach. You were sleeping when I left.'

'I sensed you weren't in the house when I woke up.'

'So you missed me, then?'

'I didn't say that. I just didn't want you to leave without saying goodbye.'

'I would not have left without telling you I intended to go…nor would I have absconded without paying my bill.'

Her mouth dropping open, Jenny stared at Rodrigo in amazement. 'You don't think I'm going to charge you for your stay when all you've done since you walked in here is look after me?'

'That was hardly your fault. Besides…' his hand scraped through his windblown black hair, then down over his jacket '…it's a business your friend is running here, *querida*—not a charity.'

At the apt reminder Jenny's heart sank. *Some helpful caretaker she'd turned out to be!* Her own business was struggling, and she had an inkling it was because her heart wasn't really in it. When she returned to London she would throw herself into things a bit more determinedly, but what if she just wasn't cut out to run a business at all? Ostensibly her talents lay in her creativity, not making money.

Thinking back over what she'd had to deal with in the past as far as her relationships were concerned, she wished she could have been stronger. But her trust had been shattered both by her brother and Rodrigo, and she'd defy anyone to cope with that and be full of confidence.

Glancing across at the flickering television screen, Rodrigo slipped off his jacket and threw it onto a cream pin-tucked armchair. Even at a distance Jenny scented the tang of the sea that clung to him from his walk. She wished she'd been well enough to accompany him.

'What are you watching?' he asked interestedly.

'Pride and Prejudice.' She swallowed down the regret that washed over her. All she'd ever really desired was a kind, loving husband, children of her own and a lovely home. A wistful sigh escaped her at the story unfolding on the screen, where she knew the heroine Lizzie *would* get the man and the house she dreamed of. 'I love period dramas...the clothes, the beauty of the architecture, the manners...and the simmering unspoken passions underneath all that buttoned-up corsetry and politeness.'

The phrase 'buttoned-up corsetry' made Rodrigo wince. He was having trouble enough trying to keep his desire for Jenny under tight control without being taunted by images of her in an old-fashioned virginal white corset—that he, of course, would be only too eager to divest her of...

'And is Mr Darcy your idea of the perfect man, Jenny?'

Her blue eyes looked dreamy for a moment, but then she shook her head. 'Not really.' Her fingers plucked restlessly at the plaid wool blanket. 'After all, he's just a character in a book. If you really lived with a man like that I'd bet it wouldn't be long before his true colours emerged. He'd probably prove to be exactly what she originally thinks him to be—an egomaniac who believes it is his God-given right to have exactly what he wants including a wife who reflects his pompous vision of himself! It's been my experience that men are selfish creatures, on the whole. They only really want what *they* want…no matter how much it may hurt the women who care for them.'

Rodrigo winced. He knew instantly this wasn't just about the fictional Mr Darcy. 'I'm sorry your experience of men has been so negative,' he murmured.

Tugging the blanket up around her chest, she visibly shivered. 'I'm not just referring to you. My brother Tim was an addict… You didn't know that, did you? You name it, he was hooked on it. Pot, cocaine, heroin, alcohol, gambling—everything. And when his own money wasn't enough to pay for it all, he thought it his right to demand mine. Especially after you and I parted and he thought I was rich.'

'I had my reservations about your brother, but I had no idea he was as you say. I wish you could have shared that with me when we were together.'

'Why? You couldn't have changed him. If you'd got to know him he'd only have ended up using you for what he could get…just like he did with me. It didn't matter that we were brother and sister.'

'What happened before he went to Scotland, Jenny? I want to know.'

She stared at him with a haunted look. 'He put me through hell, trying to get our family house from me.' She dropped her head onto her raised knees. Glancing up again, she pushed back her hair. 'When I finally agreed to buy him out, that and the legal costs almost bankrupted me. The court case was horrendous. He persuaded a besotted rich girlfriend to pay for some whiz-bang lawyer, and the lies he told about me to plead his case were vile…such vindictive, terrible lies that I wanted to die. Anyway, when I was worn out with fighting I agreed to a settlement. I only did it because I knew if he won the case everything my parents had worked so hard for would have been sold for a song to pay for his out-of-control lifestyle. Ironic that not long after he'd been paid out the house caught fire and burned down and it all went anyway.'

'My God! If I had had any idea that that was the situation you were returning to when we broke up I would have—'

'You would have what, Rodrigo? Taken me back?' Her eyes glittering, Jenny shook her head. 'I don't think so. Besides…I can fight my own battles.'

'You are strong, that is true… But it grieves me to hear you went through that alone.'

Switching off the television, Rodrigo lowered himself onto the end of the couch. His glance alighted on Jenny's lovely face as fervently as a ship looked for the lodestar—and he saw that her gaze shimmered with tears.

'The truth is I don't know if I have the heart to continue with my business' she confessed. 'I worked so hard at it—and for what? The thing I wanted most in the world was a family and a home of my own. You and I only lasted a year, my parents are gone, and my relationship with my brother is non-existent because of what happened. I never envisaged spending the rest of my life alone.'

'And neither will you be alone for ever, Jenny. It simply is not possible. One day everything will change for the better and you will have your dream.'

'Does your famous intuition tell you that Rodrigo?'

Fielding the swathe of pain that cut through him at the despondency in her voice, Rodrigo struggled to find the words to convince her life would improve. It didn't help that he had played a big part in making her mistrust her future.

'It's no surprise that you got ill. There is too much hurt and unhappiness weighing down your heart, and I honestly regret that.'

Jenny stared at him. 'I think you do. But, like me, you can't help how you're made. Your past has shaped you too, and you've grown to believe that work is the most important thing. I don't like the idea of you being alone for the rest of your life either.'

'Maybe I deserve to? Anyway, I will just have to live with my mistakes, if that's what they are.'

'Sometimes you're far too hard on yourself—do you know that?'

When she leaned over and squeezed his arm, Rodrigo sensed such a tide of heat and longing sweep over him that all he could do was stare down at that small perfect palm circling his wrist without any words at all. Then his brain engaged properly.

'I'm a man who goes for what he wants and gets it, Jenny. To get on in this life you have to cultivate some steel. To this day I've never allowed sentiment to get in the way of making the decisions that suit *me* best—whether that's in my private life or my work. You know that to your cost. So please don't waste your time thinking I need kindness and forgiveness.'

CHAPTER SEVEN

RODRIGO was on his feet before Jenny had a chance to respond. 'It's getting late, and I should see to our meal. Finish watching your DVD...relax and enjoy it.'

Without glancing back to gauge her expression, he strode out through the door into the hallway. The cat followed him. In the kitchen, he automatically located the ingredients he needed for their meal from the fridge and the larder, pausing briefly to fill a dish of food for Cozette when her pitiful mewing became too loud to ignore. Straightening, he leant his hip against the counter, pressing his fingers deeply into his brow.

It was about time Jenny fully realised that he couldn't pursue a relationship with her for a second time. Even if that meant that next time he met her eyes they would be even more wary and sad around him.

If he hadn't been married to her before would he have stayed and played nursemaid as he had done? It was an uncomfortable thought, but a truthful one at least. He'd stayed purely because it was Jenny. On Monday he was leaving, all being well, and right now he needed to employ some of that distance he spoke about. God knew it should be second nature to him when it came to relationships—especially when someone threatened to get too close. But twice now Jenny had almost made him forget that. If he employed his usual strategy it would make it less hard for him to go and easier for Jenny to let him.

A long time ago his father had warned him not to let his focus stray from his ambition. 'Play by all means,' he had advised his son. 'But do not allow yourself to become too involved.' Having made the error once before of thinking he could have it all— marriage *and* a successful business—Rodrigo intended to steer well clear of such a dangerous and misleading temptation again.

In the charmingly decorated living room, with its gently ticking French antique clock, Jenny was asleep. About to shake her, Rodrigo saw that she slumbered as deeply and peacefully as an untroubled child— just as if she'd laid all her worries and cares aside. Her angelic features were slightly flushed, and her glorious hair tumbled round her shoulders in shining ringlets the hue of golden summer sunshine.

It seemed heartless to wake her to tell her that a meal was ready. Instead he divested her of the blanket tucked round her, then lifted her carefully into his arms. She barely even stirred. Just disconcertingly rested her head against his chest and gently sighed.

Clenching his jaw, because her soft, pliant body was exquisitely, painfully arousing him, Rodrigo carried her upstairs to bed. Leaving the door slightly ajar, to let the light flood in from the landing, he didn't bother to switch on the lamp. The rose scent from her skin sneaked captivatingly under his radar. It stormed his senses as he laid her down under the covers. With great care he removed her already opened dressing gown, then dropped it onto a nearby chair.

As he leaned over to tuck the covers up round her shoulders, Jenny's stunning blue eyes fluttered open. 'Mmm...' she breathed, coiling her arms round his neck. 'You smell so nice.'

He froze. She must be dreaming he thought. But then she laid her hand across his cheek, tenderly stroking it.

'You're such a good man, really...and sometimes... sometimes so hard to resist.'

'Do you know what you are saying?' he demanded huskily.

'Yes, I do. I'm wide awake, Rodrigo.'

'This is a dangerous game you're playing, Jenny Wren.'

'Don't you want to kiss me?' she whispered, her hand moving gracefully from his cheek into his hair.

His blood heating violently, Rodrigo gripped her shoulder. Self-control was suddenly frighteningly thin. 'I want much more than just a sweet, drowsy little kiss, my angel. Unless you are prepared for that, then we will stop this right here, right now.'

In answer, Jenny gazed up at him with her bewitching light eyes full of longing. Then, with a fleeting bold smile, she slanted her petal-soft lips against his.

Kissing her back fully on the mouth was like coming home at last. His fantasy of tasting her like this again was like a pastel watercolour compared to vividly sensuous passionate reality. With a rough groan, Rodrigo let his hard, sensually aching body fall against the inviting feminine curves beneath him. His lips clashed urgently with Jenny's for a short-lived second before his tongue hungrily invaded the hot purse of the sweetest silken mouth he'd ever tasted. He devoured it like a pauper at a banquet.

Arching her body to get closer, she feathered soft little gasps of pleasure over him, and as he pressed her deep down into the mattress she matched every groan and feverish demand he was meting out with equal ardour. Her small hands urgently pushed at his sweater, in search of the warm hard flesh underneath, and she tangled her long bare legs with his still jean-clad ones.

Rodrigo was left in no doubt that they were of a single mind. Sweeping the counterpane aside so he could join her in bed, he shucked off his expensive Italian loafers, jettisoned his sweater, and repositioned himself on top of her. Then he feverishly manoeuvred Jenny's simple white nightgown up over her pale thighs until his palms located her firmly defined satin hipbones. Stilling for just a moment, he unzipped his fly.

It was as if he'd left his mind at the door. Pure, undiluted primal desire was what was driving him— desire sharpened into dizzying focus by Jenny's seductive hot mouth brushing against his over and over. Her hands were moulding themselves to his jean-clad rear as she impelled him urgently towards her.

'You have bewitched me without even trying,' he breathed against her ear, and then, freeing himself, he inserted his hard aching shaft deeply between her slender thighs in a long shattering thrust. Secluded by the semi-dark, they stared back at each other in mutual wonderment.

If this was a dream then Jenny wanted it to go on for ever… It was true she *had* been lost in the most delicious sensual fantasy about Rodrigo when she'd sensed him lift her up from the couch. The warm, woody scent of him along with the colossal strength in his arms had made that fantasy blossom into the most vividly detailed erotic sequence she could have imagined.

Then she had opened her eyes, felt his warm breath on her face, and been so transfixed by the most tempting magnetic sea of ebony silk that she hadn't had a prayer of resisting.

She could fool herself by pretending she was

delirious because of her illness, or that as a result
of her fever she wasn't yet in her right mind—but
both would be a lie. Jenny knew *exactly* what she
was doing—and why. She wanted Rodrigo more
than she'd ever wanted him. Two years apart hadn't
quelled that desire.

The Spaniard had intoxicated her senses from the
moment he'd stepped up to her at the Savoy and so
charmingly asked to know her name and if she'd like
to have dinner with him. And when he'd stepped into
Lily's guesthouse from out of the rain and then come
to her rescue when she'd fallen ill—well...she was
so *drunk* on whatever magic he'd conjured up that
she could barely think straight. Even in the throes
of raging fever she'd ached to be loved by him once
more. *Now she had her wish.*

Although Rodrigo's kisses were greedily burning, he gulped at her as if he was drinking from the
rejuvenating crystal waters of a life-giving well—as
if every taste of her was too precious to spill even a
drop. Moving deeply inside her, his magnificently
taut male body rocked Jenny to the furthest reaches
of her soul. He'd helped take care of her when illness
had struck her down, even postponing his meeting.
He had never done that before. Now, incredibly, he
was meeting another great need. A need to be held
and loved by him once again—a need that she'd
feared would never be met again.

Rodrigo had talked about maintaining distance
as friends... Surely he couldn't want to put distance

between them a second time after a union as profoundly magnetic and unforgettable as this?

Cupping her hands round his arrow-straight hips,
Jenny took him even deeper, locking her legs round
his hard-muscled back. 'Is this good for you?' she
breathed, catching a glimmer of surprise in his
eyes.

'Is this *good*? You underestimate your powers of
seduction, my angel. Right now my body, my heart,
my soul—they are all lost to you.'

Although his words touched Jenny deeply, his
smile was as sinfully delicious as a taste of decadent
chocolate ice cream in the middle of a strict diet. *The
kind a girl would willingly put on a couple of pounds
for...*

He began to thrust harder and deeper, making
Jenny cry out as he bent his head to nip the hotly
tingling tips of her breasts with the edges of his teeth,
then soothed them with the heat from his hot damp
mouth. The dammed up feelings building inside her
burst violently free. Surely the barrier restraining
them had been guarded only by the slimmest of
gossamer threads? As soon as she had wound her
arms round Rodrigo's neck she had started to come
undone...the incredibly seductive scent of his body
was enough to do that alone.

A ragged cry left her throat as wave after wave of
rapturous sensation bombarded her. Her heart hammering, Rodrigo's name was suddenly a heartfelt
mantra of unimagined joy on her lips. Shockingly,

twin rivulets of tears seeped from the corners of her eyes, mingling with the joy and pleasure. The sheer magnitude of her emotions overwhelmed her—as if every deep wound and fear she'd stored away inside her heart had suddenly surfaced at once. But Jenny scarcely had time to dwell on that as Rodrigo shivered in her arms and convulsed. Holding onto the broad, magnificent slopes of his hard male shoulders, she registered the scalding spurt of his vigorous male seed seeking its home inside her.

What have you done, Jenny? It simply wasn't like her not to think about something as vital as protection. But right then, with her body feeling so loved and languorous and her head still a little woozy from her bout of sickness, she somehow didn't care.

Resting his head on her shoulder, Rodrigo murmured something vehement in Spanish. Judging by the tone, it sounded pretty much as if he was berating himself for the same thing.

He propped himself up on an elbow, his dark gaze serious. 'I would be lying if I said I didn't know what got into me to make love with you without taking precautions, Jenny... But I want you to know I'm profoundly sorry for compromising you like this.'

'Is that all you have to say about what we just shared, Rodrigo?' Lightly, Jenny wove her fingers through the glossy sable strands of his hair.

'No.' He caught her hand, then brushed his lips across her knuckles, his expression intense. 'It is not all I have to say at all. What we just shared was incredible, wonderful...*beyond* wonderful. You are a lovely, generous, sexy woman, Jenny. Already you've made sure that I'll never forget you.'

Her heartbeat jumped in dismay. 'If you're talking about leaving then please don't. What I want right now is just to savour these precious moments we've got together without thinking about anything that makes me sad.'

'You were crying. I saw tears in your eyes.' Tracing the outline of her mouth with his forefinger, he dragged her plump lower lip downwards for a moment.

'It was overwhelming...the way you loved me. You touched feelings that I'd suppressed for a long time. Something inside me broke open, Rodrigo...something that I've held back for far too long. I feel—' Suddenly self-conscious, Jenny turned away from his intense ebony glance. 'I feel cleansed, somehow.'

'So you will sleep much better tonight. No bad dreams will come to visit you again, hmm?' Rolling over onto his side he laid his bare arm protectively across her middle.

'You'll keep them away for me,' she agreed.

Just hearing him say that the bad dreams wouldn't come made Jenny feel safe. But with her head still feeling achy and hot she sensed her body succumbing to another helpless wave of tiredness. Sighing, she snuggled down deeper into the bed. Under the covers, Rodrigo's hand moved possessively over her bare hip.

Registering the sensuous tug in her solar plexus, along with the surge of heat in her breasts, Jenny smiled. 'That's nice.'

'I have even more nice things to show you if you want.'

'You do?' *Just the anticipation made her feel boneless.*

'But there is something I need to do first.'

'What's that?'

'Sit up for me a minute.'

'Why?'

'So many questions... Have you never heard that sometimes you just need to go with the flow?'

Jenny obediently scooted up, and without pre-amble found her nightdress expertly pulled up over her head and flung to the side. Her skin prickled with goosebumps at the hot appreciative glance Rodrigo shamelessly submitted her to. His slow burning gaze all but devoured her.

'You are like an exquisite painting of a fairy queen come to life,' he said huskily. 'Perhaps I have dreamed you up?'

'I'm no dream, Rodrigo. I'm fallible flesh and blood, just like you. If I was a dream then I couldn't be hurt, could I?' She heard the catch in her voice.

Unperturbed by her comment, Rodrigo shrugged his shoulders and smiled. 'I don't care what you say. You'll always be my favourite fantasy...the one I'll summon when I'm alone in my bed at night after a hard day and need reminding of something beautiful.'

Not liking his reference to being alone, and the scene it conjured up of him being back in Barcelona without her, Jenny shivered. Desolate, she folded her arms over her chest. 'I'm cold, Rodrigo.'

'Then lie down with me, *querida*, and let me put the heat back into your blood to keep you warm...'

'Maldita sea!' He could hardly credit his clumsiness. That was the second mug he'd managed to break that morning. Sweeping the broken remnants into a dustpan, Rodrigo impatiently deposited them into the bin. Then he reached up to the overhead pine cupboard with its meticulously arranged shelves of bright painted crockery for another one.

He groaned as a tight muscle in his back stretched a little too abruptly. Strenuous exercise never fazed him. When all was said and done he was a man in the peak of fitness—even if lately his body *had* sometimes felt fustratingly fatigued. But last night he'd been making love to Jenny until the early hours of the morning. *And the more he'd demanded of her body, the more he'd craved.* It seemed as if his impossible desire was never sated.

His hand stilled on the coffee percolator's handle. It pricked his conscience that he might have selfishly taken advantage of her when she was not totally well, but she had more than matched his passion, he recalled. The memory of her soft inner thighs clamped round his middle instantly hardened him. He hissed out a ragged breath. The sooner he returned to work the better. He was quickly realising that the longer he stayed, the more this white-hot lust and longing for Jenny would consume him...no doubt to the detriment of his ability to think straight, concentrate on his work and all he had set out to uphold and achieve. *Just as his father had warned him it would.*

'Is there any of that coffee going begging? I can't tell you how good it smells.'

Rodrigo spun round. Jenny stood in the doorway, dressed in light blue denims and a sweatshirt that was just a shade darker than her eyes. The picture she made was stunning and fragile at the same time.

Rodrigo's heart lurched. 'What are you doing up? I told you to rest.'

'I'm sick of resting. I need to be up and about again or I'll go mad. Let me pour the coffee. I can do that much at least.'

Seeing her hand tremble as she reached for the coffee jug, he tutted. 'You are your own worst enemy—you know that? I'd almost forgotten how impatient you are.'

'I've lots of faults, that's true.'

'Come here.'

'Why?' She blinked owlishly at him.

He let her finish pouring the coffee, then pulled her into his arms. Everything about her delighted him...her slim compact body, sunshine gold hair, flawless blue eyes and pale satin skin.

Outside, a light rain fell onto the greenhouse roof and the neat flowerbeds alongside it. The air had a real crisp, cold bite to it. In an attempt to cool his ardour—as well as help distract a mind that seemed intent on dwelling on one thing and one thing only—Rodrigo had already been out walking, and the icy temperature had made him glad to return inside. It had also made him ache momentarily for the sunshine of Barcelona. But standing here with his arms wrapped round a sweetly scented Jenny he felt warm as toast and—not surprisingly—*aroused*.

'I want to kiss you good morning,' he murmured, lowering his face to hers.

Jenny ducked her head out of the way. 'You've already kissed me a hundred times this morning.' She grinned, her cheeks turning charmingly pink. 'I just hope you don't catch what I've had—then you'll be sorry!'

'Never.' He feigned a disapproving look. 'I would never be sorry for kissing you. It would be worth being struck down for a few days just to have had the chance to sample your irresistible charms again, my angel.'

'But then you wouldn't be able to go to your meeting and I'd have to look after you.'

'How tedious for you.' Rodrigo tried to hide his automatic resistance to the idea but failed.

'Why do you think that would be tedious for me?' A tiny concerned crease appeared between Jenny's neatly arched brows, 'I would relish every minute of it, Rodrigo.'

'And you would do it just because you have a naturally caring instinct, and not for any gain?'

'What gain? What are you talking about?'

'Wanting more of me than I can give.'

Unable to hide her alarm, Jenny stiffened in his arms.

CHAPTER EIGHT

'IF I TOOK care of you while you were ill it wouldn't be for any ulterior motive, Rodrigo. It would merely be because I care about you. Do you have a problem with that?'

All desire for coffee had fled. Jenny felt as if her stomach had a dead weight inside it at the suspicion and pain mirrored in her ex-husband's silky dark eyes.

Abruptly removing his arms from round her waist, he moved away, leaving her feeling as if she'd gone from summer to winter in one fell swoop.

'I don't want you to care about me.' A muscle flinched at the side of his jaw. 'I'd like us to part as friends, of course, but—'

'What?'

'When I leave it's best if you just forget about me. The commitment I have to my work is heavy. As I explained, that's why our marriage couldn't work. At least I was honest with you. A man like me hasn't the right to pursue a serious relationship when he knows that because of his dedication to business there's a high probability it will fail.'

'You must have been hurt very badly somewhere along the line to make you believe that—to believe that any attempt at a committed relationship would fail.'

'No!'

His denial was fierce. Jenny stepped back in alarm.

'Just because I happen to prefer concentrating my time and energy on making a success of my work doesn't mean that someone hurt me. The reality is that I'm aware of the false promises a relationship can breed...the false hope. Look around you—how many relationships do you see that even survive? I prefer to focus on something with a higher rate of success... something that does deliver on its promise.'

'And work can fulfil every hope, every dream of happiness, can it?'

'For me, right now, it gives me exactly what I want.'

'That sounds to me like somebody *did* hurt you, Rodrigo—or at least poisoned your mind about what can be possible as far as relationships go.'

'*Dios mio!* How have we got onto this tedious subject?'

Moving restlessly, as if his skin was suddenly too tight to contain whatever emotions were flooding him, the handsome Spaniard fixed her with a cold glare. Jenny held her ground.

'I know that we broke up and things didn't work out, but it wasn't because I didn't at least *try* to make it a success! But you- you decided not to try at all. What we had was really beautiful...have you forgotten that? And you just threw it away as if it meant nothing at all. I've thought about things a lot, lying ill in bed, and I know that for me life would be pretty meaningless if there was never anyone else to share it with.'

'To look after, you mean?'

'To take care of your husband and family isn't something to be ashamed of.' Inside her chest, Jenny's heart thudded hard. 'You talk as if it is.'

'You are right.' His expression surprisingly softening, Rodrigo nodded. 'Just because I have some issues about relationships, it doesn't mean that I think *you* shouldn't go for what you want, Jenny. A woman like you was not created to be alone. I know that instinctively.'

Stepping closer, he reached out to circle her waist again. Then, dipping his head, he gently brushed his mouth against hers. More than any of the passionate kisses she had received from him, that tender little kiss made Jenny's heart ache as if it had been cut in two...all the more because she tasted *goodbye* in it.

'How could I not wish anything but that all your dreams come true? I'm already envious of the man you'll eventually marry. When he gets a taste of your love and care he'll know what an angel he's fallen in love with.'

'And you, Rodrigo?' Tenderly laying her palm against his bronzed sculpted cheek, Jenny felt the pain in her heart constrict her voice to barely above a whisper. 'You're absolutely sure that you don't want my love and care?'

'I don't deserve it. And that's not because I'm feeling sorry for myself. I'm purely being realistic. And at the end of the day I'm too selfish to put someone else's welfare before myself, as you do. I tried to make our relationship work, but something in my make-up just wouldn't let me make it the priority it should have been. I've hurt you once already, Jenny... don't let me hurt you again.'

Sensing his stubbornness in clinging to such a damaging conviction, she swallowed hard. 'I can hardly equate what you're saying with how you've been towards me since you've been here. Now that we've been able to spend some proper time together without your work getting in the way, I can't imagine a man more thoughtful and caring...and, yes, unselfish. You could have left at any time, but you didn't. It's just not true that you're too self-obsessed to put someone else before yourself. I've seen a different side to you these past few days, Rodrigo...a side that really makes me hopeful.'

'Well, you should guard against that, because you'll only end up disappointed again.'

Fielding the huge swell of distress that welled up inside her, Jenny broke free of Rodrigo's hold. Reaching for her mug of coffee, she carried it across to the table. As she sat down she immediately sensed Cozette brush up against her ankles. Because she was so upset, she didn't gather the purring cat onto her lap as usual. Instead her glance alighted earnestly on Rodrigo's handsome yet troubled face, and it struck her hard that there were more shadows etched into those sublime angles and features than happiness.

'You claim the man I've spent the past few days with is too selfish to care for others? We're talking about the man who postponed an important business meeting to take care of his ex-wife—a man who sat beside her sickbed all night in a hard chair in preference to going to his own comfortable bed—a man who cooked for her and washed her hair. The same man who's so convinced only his work can bring him the happiness he craves. I think I need enlightening here, Rodrigo, because I'm honestly confused.'

Even before he opened his mouth Rodrigo despised himself for what he was about to say. Behind his hammering heart a small voice mocked: *You know what you're about to throw away again don't you?*

'To start with, I think you're deluding yourself about what I could potentially be like. This is a unique situation. We were brought together by the storm and by your sudden illness. In normal circumstances I *would* have put the demands of my business first. I'm not going to lie to you about that. I run a multi-million-pound international hotel chain that demands my input to ensure its continued success. I've worked extremely hard to get where I am—to enjoy the rewards it brings—and my aim is to continue to work hard. And, secondly, do you think I would have stayed on to take care of you if that old attraction between us hadn't flared up again? I'm only human, Jenny…even *I* can't resist the potent allure of sex.'

With her hands folded on the table, Jenny raised her stunned blue gaze to his. 'Is that all this meant to you…? A convenient opportunity to assuage your lust? I can hardly believe you could be so cruel.'

'I just want you to know the truth.'

'The truth… Yes, I realise that must be a real priority with you—especially when you stood beside me in front of the registrar and repeated your marriage vows as if they meant something. Clearly now I know they meant nothing to you at all. You should have told me from the beginning you were only here under duress. It would have been better if you'd just braved the roads and driven away to find another place to stay. It certainly would have been better for *me*!'

Feeling as if his words had hammered nails into his own coffin, Rodrigo grimaced. 'When I said my marriage vows I meant them. But sadly time and a large dose of reality proved me wrong,' he murmured. 'I should never have asked you to marry me in the first place. That *was* selfish of me.'

'Yes, it was, Rodrigo. It was selfish and cruel when probably all you wanted to do was have a brief sexual liaison without any inconvenient emotional strings attached.' Rising to her feet, Jenny hugged herself, as though fending off any more potentially hurtful blows. 'Well…in the light of all you've just told me I think it would be best if you just packed your things and left. You're probably itching to get back to work anyway. There's no need for you to stay here until Monday. I certainly don't want you staying out of any sense of obligation. In any case, I'm feeling more or less back to my normal self now, and I can't stay in bed indefinitely…not when I've a million and one things to do to get this place shipshape before Lily comes home.'

'Jenny—'

'What?'

She was withdrawing…shutting herself off from him with devastating intention, Rodrigo saw. The realisation put him in turmoil, even though he knew he was the cause.

'I promised I'd stay until Monday, and you are not right yet—I can see that. To reassure you, I'm not staying out of a sense of obligation or duty. It makes sense for you to take the next couple of days to fully get your strength back before you throw yourself into work again.'

'And you're suggesting that out of the goodness of your heart, are you? Forgive me if I can't quite believe that.'

At the door, her glance was scathing. Yet within the bitterness of her tone Rodrigo thought he heard sorrow, and regret too. His chest was so tight that he unconsciously rubbed his palm across it.

'You should just go on your way, Rodrigo, and do whatever's best for you. Put this whole inconvenient episode behind you and get back to the world you're clearly much more comfortable with. That's my advice to you.'

With her head held high, Jenny left him alone with his own morose thoughts...

Throwing herself back into taking care of things was what she had decided to do. If her body ached, or her head suddenly swam with heat, Jenny determinedly ignored it. She couldn't afford to be ill any longer.

Rodrigo had wounded her with his cruel words and the candid admission that the only reason he'd stayed to take care of her was because of the sexual attraction that had brought them together in the first place and his hope of having his lust fulfilled. Well, she had definitely contributed to helping him achieve *that* ambition. But—even though she was disappointed in him, as well as mad at herself for falling so hard for him again—Jenny found she couldn't regret the making love part. *It had been the realisation of a dream she had long held to hold him in her arms again.*

Now that he was leaving it would be all she had to console her over the harsh winter months back in London. Winter months during which she would try hard to keep her spirits up even as she worked at a career she'd lost heart in pursuing with any conviction, living in a small, cheerless rented flat because she'd lost the home she'd taken such pride in to a malevolent fire.

Seeking to drown out her despairing thoughts, she switched on the vacuum cleaner, running the machine up and down the hall carpet as if her life depended on it. Poor Cozette ran for cover at the frenetic, noisy activity, disappearing upstairs as swiftly as a bullet from a gun.

A short while later Rodrigo passed her in the hallway while she was working. But he barely glanced at her before he too ascended the staircase, presumably going up to his room to pack. Biting her lip, Jenny blinked back the scalding tears that surged into her eyes.

She was busy dusting the heavy oak sideboard in the living room when he appeared again. Sensing the aloof air that cloaked him, Jenny shivered. She saw that he was wearing his expensive raincoat—the one that had dripped onto the raffia mat that end-of-the-world stormy night—and knew with a heavy heart that nothing but sorrow lay ahead of her.

'So you're leaving, then?'

Pursing his well-cut lips, he nodded. 'It's not the way I would have liked to say goodbye, Jenny... whether you believe me or not. But it seems I have no choice, seeing as you've more or less told me to go. Can I settle my bill?'

You could say you refuse to leave me this way!
You could say you've changed your mind. Do you
think I wouldn't forgive you?

'Of course.' She made herself walk across the
carpet and out through the door ahead of him. But
she felt like an automaton because her senses were
so numbed by grief.

Pausing by the chestnut bureau in the hall that
accommodated the telephone and the reservations
book, she glanced up at Rodrigo with a frown.

'What am I doing? I said I wouldn't charge you.
You don't have to pay anything.'

'And I told you how I felt about that.' He proffered
a gold Mastercard.

Staring at it dumbly for a few seconds, she registered the reminder that he owned a multi-million-
pound business.

'Just because you've got money it doesn't mean
you should always pay. You looked after me when
I was sick and I'm very grateful. This is my way of
saying thank you.'

'I've had shelter here too, as well as eaten your
food!' His velvet-dark gaze flashed unrestrained
impatience.

Distress welling up inside her at his antagonis-
tic tone, Jenny smoothed a shaky hand across her
ponytail. 'I don't want to argue about this. Please...
just accept your stay here as a gift. I'm sure you're
impatient to be on your way and get back to work.
Here's a map of the area in case you need it.' She

returned the credit card, along with a slim folded map. 'Where will you go after your meeting here?'

'Back to Barcelona.'

After shoving both items she'd given him carelessly into his coat pocket, to Jenny's surprise he captured her hand. Her heart began to race wildly.

'It's been incredible, seeing you again. I'll never forget it. Looking after you…being in this peaceful place… It provided a rest I badly needed—even though there were a couple of nights when I must have aged about a hundred years because your fever was bad. I know I said that I only stayed because of my attraction for you, Jenny, but I promise you…there was not one second when I wished I was somewhere else.'

Her long-lashed summer-blue eyes regarded him gravely. 'At one point you told me your body, heart and soul were lost to me. I know you only said it in the throes of passion, so was that a lie too?'

It took Rodrigo a couple of moments to field the anguish that deluged him and regain his composure. 'It was no lie. When I said it, I meant it. I've never said such things to any other woman before or since you. I also meant our wedding vows when I made them, and truly regret that I couldn't keep them.'

'And yet now you can leave so easily? Without even the merest suggestion that we might see each other again?'

'I would willingly see you again, but whether it would be a good idea or not is debatable. My schedule is so crazy, and you know how much I have to travel. I wouldn't want to make you any promises I couldn't keep. I wouldn't want to let you down a second time.'

'Don't worry about it. It's okay. We had a nice time together, even though I was ill, and we'll part as friends… Is that what you want to hear?'

In answer, Rodrigo pressed a light kiss to her scented cheek and let go of her hand. He stooped to pick up his laptop case and slipped the leather strap over his shoulder. 'I hope you won't stay angry with me for ever. I hope one day you can forgive me. Don't overdo things. Please take my advice and get some more rest. *Adios*, my beautiful Jenny Wren.'

He hardly knew where he was driving—just followed the instructions to take him to Penzance from the now functioning satellite navigation system which had gone askew in the storm. It was as if he was on automatic pilot.

Verdant fields, hills, quaint Cornish villages and breathtaking beaches that were a Mecca for devoted surfers passed him by in a barely registered blur. In his mind all Rodrigo saw was Jenny's dazzling tear-washed blue gaze and the slight rosy flush to her cheeks that her illness had left behind. She was the most incredible woman…*too* incredible for a lost cause like him to even imagine having a meaningful relationship with. He could see her again, yes, and for a few short weeks, months—even a year—things might go well. But sooner or later Rodrigo's addiction to his work plus his insatiable desire for greater and greater success would bear down on him *and* Jenny, and then she would despair of him, start to mistrust him, and finally declare she had had enough and leave.

Slamming the heel of his hand against the steering wheel, he spared himself nothing with his vehement curse. Then, blinking dazedly at the map flashing on the sat nav, he saw that it showed he was now entering Penzance.

CHAPTER NINE

JENNY bade an affectionate goodbye to her reju-venated friend Lily, then returned to London and unexpected good news. There was a cheque in the post from the insurers in answer to her claim for her house.

Having waited a long time for the situation to be resolved, she now found the amount exceeded all her hopes. It meant she had a real chance to start again—to maybe buy another property, expand her business, or do whatever she wanted for a while without stress-ing about income.

However, nothing could make up for Rodrigo walking away. She knew that. Not when every morning she woke to the stark possibility that she might never see him again. Just the thought was like a dagger in her breast. Her senses had been in a state of frozen animation since he'd left. Before when she'd been with him she'd felt everything so *intensely*. Now she felt nothing.

The one small light on the horizon was that the money she'd received would give her some much-needed options to help improve her future. She still refused to consider spending any of the settlement Rodrigo had given her, and one day if she had the chance she would see that he got back every penny. But now that she was home again her three months in Cornwall seemed like a distant dream...especially the part where on a stormy October night Rodrigo had appeared.

Suddenly her small rented flat, with its impersonal air and lack of love, seemed too small to contain her increasing restlessness, and it was in this agitated state of mind that one dismal rainy evening she did a pregnancy test because her period was overdue. When the result showed positive Jenny dropped down onto the edge of the bath in stupefied shock. Staring down at the test, she finally registered the enormity of what she was seeing. *She was carrying Rodrigo's baby inside her.* The one event she'd believed would never happen had astoundingly occurred. But what was she going to do about it? Of course he would have to know—even if he decided absolutely he wanted nothing further to do with her *or* the child. She prayed that wouldn't be so. Hadn't he more than amply demonstrated that he wasn't exactly immune to her when they were together in Cornwall?

The following afternoon she took a break from work to visit a travel agent's. With thumping heart and a dry mouth she booked flights and hotel accommodation for Barcelona. What was to stop her? she argued silently as she handed over her credit card.

Thanks to her claim, she had the funds. Only yesterday she'd wrapped up the job she'd been working on so she was perfectly free to go. And her reasons were perfectly legitimate. Not only would she benefit from the warmer climate, but she would be able to see Rodrigo again and break the news that she scarcely believed was true herself.

He was going to be a father. Their re-ignited passion in Cornwall had made a baby…

'*Buenos dias, senñorita…* What can I get you?'

'Just a glass of orange juice please…*gràciis.*'

When the smiling young waiter disappeared back inside the busy café, with its hypnotic salsa music drifting out onto the Moorish-style terrace, Jenny leaned back in her chair and flipped through her Catalan phrasebook, vowing to familiarise herself with the language she had started to learn when she was last there. But then a trickle of perspiration slid down her back inside her cotton sleeveless shirt and she shut her eyes to bask in the idyllic aromatic sunshine as the ebb and flow of other diners' conversations sounded on the air around her.

'Excuse me…but aren't you staying at our hotel?'

Jenny's eyes opened with a start at the sound of the unfamiliar American voice. A beaming masculine face with a row of impossibly white teeth beneath a neatly trimmed greying moustache loomed back at her. An enthusiastic hand was stuck out to shake hers.

'I'm Dean Lovitch and this is my wife Margaret. We arrived three days ago, same as you. We saw you at Reception but you looked a little distracted, if you don't mind me saying, and it didn't seem right to bother you just then. We've just been to visit the Sagrada Família. Have you seen it yet?'

'You mean the unfinished cathedral? I visited it once two years ago, when I was last here, but I fully intend to go again. I've been mainly taking it easy for the past few days rather than visit the tourist spots, to tell you the truth. I was rather under the weather before I came out here.'

'I'm real sorry to hear that. But it seems like a good place to come to if you're in need of a pick-me-up, don't you think? Mind if we join you? All the other tables seem to be taken.'

'Go ahead. I'm Jenny Renfrew, by the way.'

'It's good to meet you, Jenny.'

The couple sat themselves down opposite her—the tall, spaghetti-thin husband and his plump, diminutive sandy-haired wife. Straightening in her chair, Jenny vowed to be sociable. She was here for a fortnight, after all. No doubt there would be plenty of other warm sunny afternoons in which to ponder her life over a cool drink on a terrace somewhere. Besides... Dean and Margaret had the kind of faces that immediately instilled trust, she decided. Their manner was warmly considerate, and she wasn't surprised to learn that they had three grown-up children who had all 'fled the nest'—which was why they'd decided a long overdue holiday in Europe was called for to help them adjust.

'Are you here all by yourself, Jenny?' Margaret softly enquired as the waiter placed the glass of juice she'd ordered in front of her.

'I am.'

'You seem so young. Isn't there someone special who could have come with you?'

'You mean like a boyfriend?' Fielding the arresting vision of Rodrigo that swarmed into her mind, making her tummy flip over, Jenny wrapped her hands tightly round her glass. 'There's no one special in my life, I'm afraid.'

'Well, there seems to be no shortage of good-looking boys around, that's for sure.' Dean grinned. 'It's a wonder a pretty English Rose like you hasn't got at least a dozen of them lining up to ask you for a date. Perhaps you do, but you're just not telling? I'm sure your parents told you that you gotta be careful. I'm glad that I've got sons, quite frankly. I would have been prematurely grey if I'd had a daughter! Especially one that looked like you.'

'Dean, you're embarrassing Jenny.'

'Sorry, sweetheart.' He instantly apologized. 'Hey, I've just had a great idea. We were going to check out this supposedly incredible spa hotel this afternoon. Margaret thought she might book herself a massage, and I hear the grounds are spectacular. Want to come with us?'

'A spa hotel you said?' Inside her chest, Jenny's heart seemed to ricochet against her ribs.

'Yeah… It's owned by some local billionaire, so we hear, and just a few streets over. How do you feel about seeing how the other half lives for a while, Jenny?'

In the end she couldn't resist accompanying the sociable Americans. Despite choosing her accommodation because of its proximity to his star hotel, she'd put off confronting Rodrigo with her news for three days now, while she nervously rehearsed how to tell him about it in her head, but sooner or later she would have to see him.

But as soon as Jenny stepped out of the sultry heat into the air-conditioned foyer of the dazzling chrome and glass hotel and onto the sleek marble floor, with its chic contemporary furniture and coolly stylish décor, her heart started to thump and her legs turned to marshmallow.

Rodrigo was the owner of all this, she reminded herself.

Faced with the reality of his wealth again after two long years, she found it was almost too much to take in. The man who had sat by her sickbed on a hard rattan chair without so much as even one small complaint, the man who had made himself so at home in Lily's humble, quaint guesthouse was the owner of this incredibly chic, ultra-modern luxurious hotel and several others like it. It was indeed a sobering thought.

'Shall we have the grand tour?' Dean smiled, already walking towards a formidably smart receptionist who looked more like a catwalk model for some elite designer label than a hotel employee.

'You're very quiet, Jenny,' the diminutive Margaret whispered to the younger woman as they followed another stylishly uniformed receptionist up the sweeping marble staircase to the first floor, the soothing sound of water spilling gently into an indoor fountain accompanying them. 'I think I can guess how you feel... The scent of money is practically oozing out of the walls. It's a little bit overwhelming, isn't it?'

Her gaze on the modern sculpture and eye-catching art, Jenny was still struggling to articulate something conversational when she noticed twin doors opening at the end of the walkway they were traveling down. A tall, dark-haired, designer-suited male figure emerged ahead of a group of similarly attired people. *Rodrigo!* She would recognise him in a veritable *sea* of strangers.

Suddenly there was no audible sound at all apart from the loud roaring of blood rushing at a hundred miles an hour through Jenny's head. *Oh, God...don't let him see me... Please don't let him see me.* What was he going to think if he should catch sight of her? That she'd deliberately tracked him down, expecting something from him? She'd *die* if he thought that—even though she was expecting his baby.

He was holding open the door for his board members, or whoever they were. She saw that now. Seeing him glance casually towards their little group, she momentarily froze. In the same instant a sickening sense of nausea gripped her insides. What a moment for morning sickness to hit! Her intention had been to walk swiftly back down the marble staircase, hopefully unseen, and try to meet Rodrigo at some later date. But now, disconcerted by the nausea, she turned on her heel too quickly and a searing pain shot through her ankle. It made her stumble awkwardly and, unable to right herself, she completely lost her balance.

'Oh, God.' Suddenly she was in a humiliating heap on the floor, with every pair of eyes in the vicinity on *her*.

'Are you okay, honey? Are you hurt?' Margaret's American husband dropped to his haunches, his avuncular features genuinely concerned as he put a comforting arm round Jenny's shoulders.

'I think I've twisted my ankle. I turned on it too suddenly… That's just typical of me, I'm afraid.'

On the periphery of her consciousness she saw a striking-looking dark-suited male issue an urgent command and, glancing up, watched an almost choreographed seam appear down the middle of the small group of people that had quickly gathered round her, allowing the man to step to the front.

He stared down at Jenny with utter disbelief in his ebony dark gaze. 'Is it really you?' he husked.

'Yes, Rodrigo.' She sighed heavily, pushing a swathe of tumbling blonde hair out of her eyes, her humiliation and embarrassment total. 'It's me.'

'What have you done to yourself?'

'It's unbelievable, I know, but I think I've twisted my ankle.'

'Does it hurt?' He crouched to gently circle the slim joint with his hand.

Jenny immediately flinched at the dizzying sensation of pain, though she was not unaware of the intoxicating warmth emanating from his large smooth palm either.

'Yes, it hurts.' She despaired of the quaver in her voice—was terrified Rodrigo might judge her as feeble and clumsy. To be frank, she'd have quite liked a handy magic spell to make her disappear.

But now the handsome Spaniard was at ground level too, and Dean Lovitch was assessing him with definite suspicion in his eyes.

'Do you know this lady?' he demanded.

'Yes, I do. And you are?'

As if sensing the other man's authority, Dean slowly withdrew his arm from round Jenny's shoulders. 'I'm Dean Lovitch. My wife and I are staying at the same hotel as Jenny and we all came here together.'

'She will be all right now, Señor Lovitch. *I* will take care of her.'

'And your name is?'

'Rodrigo Martinez. This is my hotel.'

'Oh.' Getting swiftly to his feet, his face a little red, Dean placed his arm round his wife's shoulders, as if needing to bolster himself after the shock of learning Rodrigo's identity.

'Please...' Jenny whispered, her blue eyes imploring as she glanced into the hypnotic beam of Rodrigo's. 'Don't be concerned about me. I'll be okay in a minute. My friends will help me... As Mr Lovitch told you, I'm staying at the same hotel as them. Go back to your meeting, or whatever it is you were doing, Rodrigo. I'll catch up with you at a more convenient time.'

'You're in no position to tell me to do anything, Jenny. Not when you have been injured in my own hotel and I don't even know what you are doing here. I have a personal suite in the building. I'll take you there and then call our resident doctor to take a look at your ankle.'

Just as he'd done at Lily's, Rodrigo slid his arm beneath Jenny to lift her bodily against him. Registering a mixture of surprise and respect in the interested glances watching them so avidly, she tried to rouse herself to protest. But it wasn't easy when the sensation of being held once more in front of Rodrigo's wonderful chest, along with the warmth of his hard body, was besieging her without mercy.

'You shouldn't be taking me anywhere! Put me down, Rodrigo...please.'

'Not on your life, *querida*. Stop fighting me and just relax.'

'Want us to wait for you, Jenny?' Dean asked anxiously.

Jenny shook her head, attempting a reassuring smile in her new friends' direction. 'Don't let this spoil your visit, you two. I—I expect I'll see you later, back at the hotel.'

What would the couple make of Rodrigo's possessive 'take charge' stance when she'd categorically told them there was no one special in her life? she fretted.

Issuing some crisp instructions to a well-dressed hovering male colleague, Rodrigo swept past the gathered throng of curious onlookers with a purposeful stride towards the elevator, his strong arms supporting Jenny as though she weighed no more than the smallest child...

Lying Jenny down on the plush leather couch in the suite's sitting room, Rodrigo propped her injured ankle carefully up on some satin cushions. Carrying her from the hall downstairs to the elevator, then up to the suite, had been like an exquisite form of masochism. He had felt every sweet contour of her body beneath her simple summer clothes, breathed in her heat and rose-tinted scent a thousand times magnified, and whenever she'd gazed up at him with those crystalline blue eyes all he'd been able to do was fall into silence. He had missed her more than he had dreamed possible, but it wasn't something that reassured him.

What was she doing in Barcelona? Had she come to look for him? The idea all but stalled his heart, even though he knew such an undertaking was fruitless. Hadn't he made it clear enough back in Cornwall that there could be no future for them? Jenny's unexpected enchanting presence definitely raised the spectre of a familiar old fear he hardly felt equipped to deal with again.

'I'll get you a glass of water. The doctor should be with us any minute now.'

'You're always coming to my rescue.'

'Did you think I would leave you lying there in the middle of the floor? Perhaps you were hoping that some other man would come to your rescue instead?'

'What are you talking about?'

Rodrigo shrugged, not liking the dizzying surge of jealousy that gripped his guts in a vice at the idea she might even *look* at another man, let alone hope for one to rescue her. 'Did you come to Barcelona on your own, or do you have a companion? And how is it that you are here?'

She glanced at him with a distressed look. 'Yes, I came to Barcelona on my own, and no, I don't have a companion. And I'm here because I—I...'

'Yes?'

'I'm here because something has happened that I need to tell you about.'

'Did your brother come back from Scotland? Has he been bothering you again?'

'No.' Jenny sighed. 'It's not that.'

'Why did you come to the hotel instead of my apartment?'

'I didn't intentionally come here today to find you. The American couple I was with downstairs wanted to visit the hotel because they'd heard it was something special. Margaret wanted a massage, and they asked me to join them to have a look round. Now I wish I hadn't.'

'Why? Because you didn't want to see me again?'

'I didn't even know you were here! How could I know when you haven't even been in touch?' In her agitation, Jenny restlessly moved her leg off the satin cushion, grimacing as the pain in her ankle obviously registered with a vengeance.

'*Maldita`sea!* Where is that doctor?'

'I don't want to see your doctor, Rodrigo. I'd much rather you rang me a taxi so I can go back to my own hotel. I probably just need to pack some ice round my ankle and it'll be fine.'

'Don't be ridiculous.'

'I'm not being ridiculous,' she protested, huffing and folding her arms over her candy-pink shirt. 'I'm being sensible. You don't want me here—I know that. You're clearly embarrassed that I've shown up, and to top it all off in such a stupidly dramatic way too. I'm not trying to compromise you, Rodrigo, whatever you may privately think. Our meeting up again like this at your hotel is pure coincidence. Now I just want to go.'

Profoundly disturbed by the idea that Jenny would refuse any further help from him, as well as leave on bad terms, Rodrigo dropped down onto the couch beside her. Before he knew what he intended, he'd reached for her hand and brought it up to his lips. Once again the subtle but lethal rose-tinted fragrance that clung to her invaded him. Heady desire infiltrated his blood with a vengeance, searing him hotter than any desert wind might. Inside, a quiet desperation clamored to have that desire once again fulfilled. 'I didn't realise until now that I've been suffering from a faulty memory, Jenny Wren.' The smile he delivered to her widened blue eyes was unapologetically provocative.

'Meaning?'

'I thought my recollection of your beauty was unimpeachable. But now I see it was not. You're far lovelier than even *I,* who has examined you closely, could recall. When I saw you standing there with your friends I honestly believed I must be dreaming.'

Someone rapped loudly on the outer door. Biting back his intense frustration, Rodrigo rose swiftly to go and greet the resident hotel doctor.

CHAPTER TEN

THE doctor's verdict was that Jenny had suffered only a slight sprain. During the whole time that she was being examined by the smart-suited professional her mind was racing.

The startling evidence of Rodrigo's wealth and status was all around her. From the chic contemporary furniture in the fabulously designed flower-filled air-conditioned suite to the stunning art on the walls and even the timelessly elegant way he was dressed. Every tanned, whipcord-lean, hard-muscled inch of him screamed success beyond the wildest of dreams.

Even though making her mark in business had never been her main priority Jenny still felt a little insecure that she hadn't made a better go of her own venture. But the reality was that her brother's addiction and sometimes cruel conduct had sapped her energy and her emotions down to the marrow— especially when he'd instigated the court case to try and take the family home away from her. All that had been coupled with her distress at her marriage ending, and Jenny was amazed she'd been able to continue working and functioning normally at all.

As Rodrigo politely thanked the urbane doctor and then showed him out, she determinedly swung her legs to the floor. Her injured ankle had a very neat professional bandage applied round it now, but it still throbbed like merry hell. Gingerly she slid her bare foot into her flat, brown-strapped leather sandal. It didn't exactly help her confidence to feel so physically vulnerable in front of Rodrigo once more. Especially knowing she still had to tell him about her pregnancy.

'What do you think you're doing?'

The rich-accented voice at the door made her jump.

'I'm putting my sandal back on. Thanks very much for getting the doctor to see me, but I'm not intending on taking up much more of your time.'

'You said earlier that you had something to tell me?'

'I do.'

'And that is?'

As he stood there in front of Jenny, with his arms folded across the front of that elegant suit, Rodrigo's sable eyes were admonishing and yet somehow wickedly teasing too. His black hair had a burnished shine on it fierce enough to dazzle an Alps skier. Frankly, he looked like the drop-dead gorgeous cover model of an *haute couture* fashion magazine for men, and just as intimidating. When he'd helped her throw the tarpaulin over Lily's storm-threatened greenhouse he had somehow seemed far more approachable and a little less out of her league.

'I'm pregnant.'

'What?'

Jenny was glad she was sitting down. Rodrigo's stunned expression was already making her anxious. 'I did a pregnancy test when my period was late and it was positive.'

'My God.' He crossed the room to the couch where she sat. 'Why didn't you ring me straight away?'

'It's not really the kind of news you should convey over the phone, is it?' It was hard to hear herself across the sound of her galloping heart. 'I thought it was best if I came out here to see you and tell you to your face. I know you never wanted children, and the fact is we're no longer married either...but I hoped that when you heard you were going to be a father you might—you might consider the possibility of us trying again.'

Did she really have the temerity to risk suggesting such a thing? Jenny thought in disbelief. And suddenly she found herself more vulnerable in front of Rodrigo than any illness or injury could ever render her.

When he dropped down onto the end of the couch she longed to know what thoughts were dwelling behind that serious dark gaze, but she feared hearing them revealed too.

'Jenny, *querida*, I—'

She laid her hand across his. 'Don't say no straight away… Please just think about it for a while. Do you think you could do that?'

To her surprise, he moved her hand and tucked it possessively inside his.

'*Sí…* I can do that. But you have to understand what a great shock this news is to me.'

Hearing doubt and apprehension in his voice, instead of the elation she imagined most soon-to-be fathers might express, Jenny felt the hurt ebb through her, making her want to tug her hand free. However, sheer hope made her keep it where it was, resting in the delicious warmth of Rodrigo's palm.

'But not a terrible one, I hope? To have a child is the most wonderful thing, Rodrigo… I know you've always resisted the idea, but given time you might come round to seeing that it can be the most amazing blessing.'

'One thing I do know is that we cannot have you remaining at your hotel. Clearly you should stay at the apartment. I'll drive you back there myself. You can stay there with me at least until you need to go back home. That will give us plenty of time to discuss things. We can pick up your luggage on the way.'

Now she did tug her hand free. He was talking about her going home, and that wasn't what she wanted to hear at all. Telling herself that he needed time to fully absorb her news before he reached a decision about renewing their relationship, Jenny realised she had no choice but to be patient. As much as her heart ached to have Rodrigo genuinely care for her, just as she cared for him, as well as yearning for him to embrace the idea of them having a child, she would simply have to bide her time.

But it was hard when she was so in love that the depth of her feelings was like a gnawing physical ache inside her.

Her breathing hitched. Staring back into Rodrigo's sculpted handsome face, it was as though she was looking at him for the very first time. The echo of her thudding heart reverberated round her brain. 'Do you really want me to come back with you now to the apartment?' she questioned quietly. 'What about your work?'

'Did you hear me say that work was my priority today, *querida*?' His lips formed a surprisingly tender smile, the charismatic gesture charging the space and making it thrillingly intimate. Looping his arm round her shoulders, he tipped up Jenny's chin so that she was forced to meet his disturbing gaze head-on. 'Whatever else is going on, Jenny Wren…it is good to have you here.'

His warm lips brushed gently and beguilingly against hers. Jenny heard her last defence crash to the ground in a pile of rubble and smoke. Her senses were so intoxicated by him, her heart so full, how could it do anything else?

But a kiss that had started out as an affectionate caress quickly flared into something more urgent and primal as his tongue dived commandingly inside her mouth and his strong arms circled her waist to crush her to him. His hand palmed her breast. The exquisite pressure against the already throbbing sensitive tip made Jenny emit a softly ragged sigh.

Tensing, Rodrigo immediately removed his lips to stare down at her with a rueful smile. 'My apologies for taking advantage of you yet again, *querida*... especially when you're injured and hurting. But it's clear I have a tendency to temporarily lose my mind whenever I'm around you.'

She wanted to tell him it didn't matter...that he could lose his mind around her whenever he liked. But the nausea that had gripped her downstairs suddenly returned in a debilitating wave.

'Jenny?' There was definitely alarm in Rodrigo's examining ebony gaze. 'What's the matter?'

When she didn't immediately answer, because she was concentrating all her attention on not disgracing herself, he jumped to his feet and swore.

'*Maldita sea!* Clearly you are in shock after your accident. The doctor should have foreseen this... How could he have been so remiss? What was he thinking of? Let me get you some water.'

He was back in a trice, proffering a tall crystal glass. Jenny gulped down the cool, clear mineral water it contained as though it were a lifeline. A few seconds later the sickness that had so uncomfortably invaded her thankfully abated.

'It's all right. It's not shock, Rodrigo. It's just a touch of morning sickness. I'm getting used to it.'

'Oh.' He appeared to mull this over. 'The sooner I get you back to the apartment in La Ribera the better,' he announced decisively. 'Then you can rest as much as you like until you feel better.' Delving into his inside jacket pocket for his mobile, he reeled off some urgent-sounding instructions in Spanish to the person he'd called. 'My car will be at the front entrance in five minutes,' he informed her.

He'd left Jenny relaxing on the terrace beneath an umbrella, her injured ankle elevated on a chair, a fresh glass of juice and a light snack at her elbow, and returned to work. Rodrigo's plan was to finish as early as he could to rejoin her. She'd been worryingly quiet when they'd left the hotel to drive to the apartment in La Ribera—the apartment they'd once shared. Something told him it was because he hadn't acted as if he welcomed her surprising and unexpected news about the baby.

He truly regretted that, but truth to tell he'd been knocked sideways by it—as well as by Jenny showing up at his hotel as she had. The idea of becoming a father still reverberated through him like the aftershocks of a quake. Understandably, he was feeling a little dazed. Yet after their passionate night together in Cornwall he *had* worried about the possibility of such an event happening after so thoughtlessly making love to Jenny without protection. There was no question he wouldn't do the right thing by her. Their child would have everything an infant could need and more. But the impact of a child on his up-until-now independent lifestyle certainly gave him pause.

And if he'd been a bit heavy-handed about insisting Jenny stay with him at the apartment while they thrashed things out he made no apology for it. *How else could he keep an eye on her and make sure all was well?* Her complexion was still far too pale for his total peace of mind. Was the pregnancy already taking its toll on her?

Not for the first time Rodrigo found himself regretting that he'd left her that day, when she'd only just started to recover from the fever that had afflicted her. Thoughts and memories of their time together had relentlessly assailed him ever since. And sometimes during business meetings at work Rodrigo had found his attention wandering from the agenda with worrying frequency. *His father would roll over in his grave!*

Each time it had happened it had been without a doubt because he was thinking about Jenny... He was usually recalling her enchanting blonde looks, the way she always smelled so good, the way she moved her hands so gracefully to illustrate what she was saying, and most of all the way her enticingly beautiful body had felt under his again...*sublime*.

That particular stirring memory had disrupted many a good night's sleep. And the next day Rodrigo was inevitably grouchy and ill-tempered due to lack of rest.

* * *

The Barcelona apartment was situated in an impressive eighteenth century building in an area that had formerly been the preserve of the traditional fishing industry. Now it was an ultra-modern destination, packed with boutiques, chic restaurants and bars. Rodrigo himself had had a large say in the innovative interiors that occupied the building, and a couple of prestigious awards had come his way because of it. *But right now all that seemed irrelevant somehow.* The only thing that really concerned him was Jenny.

She wasn't out on the terrace where he'd left her. Cursing his inability to leave work when he'd said he would in order to be with her, he quickened his stride, thinking maybe she'd got fed up with waiting and phoned for a cab to go back to her hotel.

As he flung open all the doors in the apartment his anxiety grew. But when at last he peered into the stylish contemporary living room it was to discover Jenny, dozing lightly on one of the sumptuous white couches.

'You're back,' she said huskily, opening her eyes.

The strangest sensation seized Rodrigo... It was a heartfelt impulse to know what it might be like to come home to Jenny *every* day when he finished work...to have her say 'You're back' and not be able to hide her pleasure or joy. For a second his throat was too dry to speak.

'Did you see the sunset?' she added softly, when

he remained mute. She briefly glanced out through the opened French windows that led onto another pretty balcony. 'It's so beautiful. I can even see the spires of Gaudi's cathedral. I'd forgotten just how incredible it is.'

The dazzling amber and gold rays that flooded onto the room's burnished wood floor were *nothing* compared to the incandescent loveliness of the girl in front of him, Rodrigo thought hungrily.

Before he could stop himself he promised to take her to see the work that had been done on the cathedral since she'd last been there, before adding, 'How's your ankle?'

'A lot less painful since I took one of the painkillers your doctor left.'

'Perhaps you shouldn't take any more. You're pregnant, remember?'

'I did check with the doctor when you briefly left the room to answer the phone.' Jenny frowned. 'But of course I would be sensible about things like that.'

'I'm glad to hear it. And it's good to see that you have some colour back in your cheeks too,' he observed, unbuttoning his jacket as he moved towards her.

'Did you have another long meeting?' Drawing her legs up to the side, Jenny curved her mouth into a sympathetic smile as he sat down beside her.

'There are *always* long meetings and equally long unsocial hours when you run a business. I'm sure you remember that, since it was one of the reasons I knew it wasn't fair to you to carry on with our marriage.' He shrugged, impatiently tugging his royal blue silk tie free from his shirt collar. 'But just the same I'm sorry I didn't get back as early as I promised.'

'There's no need to apologise...I do understand.'

'You do?'

Rodrigo couldn't quite believe she meant that. He'd always been acutely aware of just how much time he spent away from home when he was working, and had been uneasy about it when he'd been married to Jenny.

'Yes, I do. You must be hungry,' she commented lightly, her summer-blue gaze dipping for a moment when he glanced steadily back at her.

'I am, but I've got into the habit of eating out most evenings when I'm here. You must also be hungry, *querida*. Shall we go out to dinner? Are you up to it?'

'I'll be fine. I've got to start putting my weight on my ankle again if I want it to get better.'

'I wasn't particularly meaning your injured ankle. I was referring to the fact that you're with child.'

Their eyes met and locked. Jenny gave Rodrigo a slow smile. 'It's not some illness, you know. I'm not going to suddenly retire from the world just because I'm pregnant!'

CHAPTER ELEVEN

'I CAN still hardly believe it.'

In one fluid, easy motion, Rodrigo got to his feet. A little anxious, Jenny watched him move to the centre of the room and then turn to face her. The last spectacular amber gold rays of the sunset turned to fiery orange before dying away completely. In its wake the room became dim and silent. Uncurling her legs, she gingerly put both feet to the floor, trying not to wince as she experimentally put some of her weight onto her bandaged ankle.

But the pain of her injury was nothing compared to the sense of desolation that was rapidly growing inside her at the idea of Rodrigo rejecting her pregnancy or thinking she was trying to manipulate him back into marriage.

'I want this baby,' Jenny said dully, folding her arms protectively across her stomach. 'I want to keep it and I will. No matter what you decide to do.'

Her throat was suddenly so tight and painful that tears were a scant breath away. But any weeping she did she resolved to do in private. It was already humiliating enough to have the father of her expected child look at her as though he'd just heard the worst news he'd ever received, without humiliating herself further by breaking her heart in front of him.

'To raise a child...' levelling his gaze, Rodrigo wiped his hand over his cheekbone '...it's best that the parents are in a stable relationship...no?'

'Ideally, I think, yes. But I know we don't live in a perfect world. People make mistakes, and sometimes it's just not possible to have a stable relationship. In that case one might decide to raise a child on one's own. I'm willing to do that, Rodrigo. If you really can't contemplate us being together any more, don't worry that I'm going to demand you support me.'

'Is this how you were with your feckless brother?'

'What do you mean?'

'I mean he demands money to feed his addictions and you simply give it to him without a fight...without standing up for yourself?'

Jenny's stomach plummeted to the ground, as though she were travelling in an out-of-control elevator. 'I didn't just *give* him the money! You have no idea how he could be. He was manipulative and cruel, and he had ways of getting what he wanted no matter how much I resisted his demands or said what I thought.' Shuddering at the memories that mercilessly flooded back, Jenny felt her eyes burn as she stared at Rodrigo. 'He used to taunt me that I wasn't a "real woman" because my marriage had failed. The fault obviously must lie with me. When insults illustrating how useless I was both as your wife and a businesswoman didn't work he used fits of pure rage to intimidate me. When that kind of thing happens more times than you care to remember your confidence in your ability to do anything can very quickly desert you, and for a while my business got into trouble because I felt so overwhelmed. I'm not proud of that. But I *am* proud of the fact that one day I woke up and took steps to end the misery—despite the horrible threats that came my way. I fought to keep the house in court, then gave Tim a more than generous price for his share of it when I won so that he could move on somewhere else. You may not know this about me, Rodrigo, but I *am* strong. Strong enough to face whatever challenges might lie ahead and not be defeated…even challenges like raising a child on my own.'

'Your worthless brother shouted at you repeatedly?'

'Yes.'

'*Cabrón!* You are well rid of him. If I had known you were returning to such a situation I would have stepped in and dealt with it once and for all.'

'I know,' Jenny sighed. 'That's why I never told you the truth about how Tim could be.'

'In any case…understand that you will *not* be raising our child on your own.'

Immediately Jenny sensed the steely resolve in his voice.

'Do you really think I would stand aside and let you do that? I may not have planned on starting a family, but that doesn't mean that I won't face up to my responsibilities. I most definitely *will*.'

A single hard-to-contain tear slid down Jenny's cheek. 'Is that the only way you view this, Rodrigo? As a kind of duty you have to fulfil?'

'My head is spinning at what you've just told me about the situation with your brother—the fact that I unknowingly let you return to such abuse. It makes me furious. But I'm sorry…I don't mean to sound so cold.' The tension in his shoulders visibly relaxing, he sat down beside her and cupped her chilled hands between his palms. 'We will reach the best solution for both the child and us—of that I am certain. Will you just allow me a little time to think things through?'

'Take as long as you want.' Too distressed to want to notice how emphatically his touch warmed her, Jenny sniffed, tugging back her hands. 'I'll give you my home phone number in England before I leave. When you've had enough time to think things over you can ring me.'

It was almost *unbearable* to be so close to the man she loved and yet feel a distance wider than the most yawning chasm. Intent on escaping to deal with her tormenting emotions in private, Jenny surged to her feet. The pain that jackknifed through her ankle almost made her cry out, but she stoically ignored it.

Before she had the chance to move away, Rodrigo

stood up beside her. Firmly turning her round to face him, he settled his hands either side of her waist. 'You are not running back to England. We'll work things out together, Jenny. Don't turn away from me…please. I don't think I could bear it.'

The desolation she saw etched in the sublime angles and planes of his beautiful face almost made Jenny catch her breath. Somewhere inside her hope leapt like a rekindled flame in a burned-low candle. 'Oh, Rodrigo…' Touching her hand to his hollowed cheek, she suddenly couldn't prevent the steady flow of scalding tears that seeped from her eyes.

Murmuring something low, Rodrigo lifted her high in his arms against his chest and stalked with her into his bedroom. In the dim half-light of the balmy evening he urgently covered Jenny with his body on the king-sized bed as though the world might end if he didn't. Then he claimed her lips again and again with hot, open-mouthed kisses as passion-driven hands tore at her clothes—removing hers, then his own, before holding her arms high above her head and linking their fingers.

As their gazes locked in the subdued evening light, with the sensual, drugging scent of late-in-the-season exotic blooms drifting up to them from the lovely gardens below, he drove himself hard into her body, his soulful dark eyes burning like the sparks of fiery embers into the walls of her heart and capturing it.

His highly charged possession registered right down to the very corners of Jenny's soul. Meeting her lover's kisses with equal mindless hunger, she felt Rodrigo's fingers press deep into her buttocks to make their bodies fit even more closely. Her senses were already drowning in the musky heat of his slick, hard-muscled male form when they were seized by her violent climax. She barely knew where the feral cry that left her lips came from, but the sea of powerful sensual release was so profoundly intense and shocking that it rocked through her like an earthquake.

Glancing up, she looked, stunned, into Rodrigo's scorching gaze. As he rose above her she recognised blazing intent as he bucked, renting the sultry air with a primeval shout of his own. And as the echoes of that heart-jolting shout died away to mere shadows he laid his dark head between Jenny's breasts, the ragged deep breaths that left his lips gradually slowing.

Letting her lids flutter closed, Jenny played softly with his hair. The dark strands were incredibly soft and silky in her hand and cried out to be touched. *If only he loved me*, she thought fervently. If only he loved our baby and me with no holds barred, as if we were the most important things in the whole world to him. Then how perfect these stunning moments would be.

But he had asked her to give him time, she recalled. And she would...she *would*.

Stirring, Rodrigo lifted his head to contemplate her with a wicked lascivious grin, before pressing his lips to her still flat, smooth-skinned stomach, deliberately letting them linger so that his heat felt like a brand. Then he glanced back at her again, and the expression in his long-lashed sable eyes made Jenny's insides cartwheel.

'It is incredible that you carry the fruit of our loving deep inside you,' he murmured, and his rich voice had a definite catch in it. 'And now you have intoxicated me like a drug, and I am indeed... addicted.'

Moving upwards again, he bent his head to suckle her rose-tipped breasts in turn, and Jenny realised that the fire which had blazed between them had embers that were all too ready to be stoked again. As he smiled into her eyes, Rodrigo's gaze was again hungry and hot.

'I'm not trying to trap you, Rodrigo...with the baby, I mean' she said softly.

'Angel, you trapped me the first moment I saw you. I have never had such a violent reaction to the mere sight of a beautiful woman before. And when I found Lily's place, on that cold and rainy night, I could hardly believe that the storm had steered me back into your presence again. But let's not talk right now...I'm too impatient for words when all I really want to do is enjoy you. Come, sit astride me, so that I can savour every beautiful inch of you.'

His big hands were careful to help her avoid hurting her ankle as they swapped positions. Then it was Jenny's turn to feast her eyes on the taut, bronzed-skinned body beneath her, with a gentle riot of curling black hair dusting his nipples, disappearing in a slim, sensual column down to his narrow-hipped pelvis. Adjusting her thighs over his, she hungrily accepted him inside her. His penetration was deep and smooth, and she moaned low and tossed her head back with the sheer wild pleasure of it. Then she started to rock a little...

'I'd like us to take a shower together before we go out to dinner,' Rodrigo told her huskily.

'What about my bandaged ankle?'

He lifted a shoulder. 'What about it? There are infinite ways we can accommodate whatever is needed, my angel.' His expression glazed with passion, he cupped Jenny's hips to rock her even harder against him. 'You can lean against me the whole time...' His breath was ragged again as he watched her move over him, her blonde hair an enticing tousled mass of corn-gold against her pale slim shoulders. 'And I can wash your hair for you, just like I did once before. I'm an expert now, remember? Then you can wash mine. Afterwards, I will redo the dressing for you.'

'Rodrigo?'

'What is it, beautiful?'

'Didn't you—?' Another helpless moan left Jenny's lips as he pushed upwards and high inside her. 'Didn't you say something about not talking?'

'*Sí*. I did. I guess you'll just have to kiss me passionately to make me stop.'

* * *

His black silk pyjama bottoms riding low on his hips, his chest bare, Rodrigo returned to the bedroom with the two cups of coffee he'd made. Last night they had agreed to give going out to dinner a miss. Instead he had ordered some food from a favourite local restaurant to be delivered, and they'd enjoyed it sitting in their robes at the huge glass table in the dining room.

Now, the sun-kissed morning light was drifting in through the large plate-glass windows, and the undrawn coffee-coloured silk curtains were moving gently either side of the frames in the breeze.

The delicate light outlined Jenny's still sleeping form. Her slim pale arms were down by her sides as she slept on her stomach in the middle of the huge canopied bed, her golden hair a riot of silk over her shoulders and her exquisitely shaped back bare to the waist.

Leaving the coffee on a bedside cabinet, Rodrigo simply stood at the side of the bed to gaze at her. Just the sight of her made the blood pound hard in his veins. And last night…last night he had been so close to confessing that he loved and adored her. *What had held him back?* She was carrying his baby, for goodness' sake!

The thought was like a small explosion inside him. Prevalent in his emotions was pride, possessiveness and joy…ecstasy, even. It hardly made sense that he couldn't voice his feelings to Jenny. But unfortunately, given his past, it *did* make sense.

Even now Rodrigo sensed his father's austere ghost looming over him—his disapproving gaze and the countless warnings he'd drummed into him about the dangers of losing his focus making him shudder. Then he thought about how his dedication to the business and his long hours away from home had doubtless contributed the unhappiness he'd seen in Jenny when they were together. Could he risk hurting her a second time? He was crazy about her. It would hurt so much more this time if things between them didn't work out...all the more because they would have a child together.

In the bed, Jenny drew her knees up under the covers, rolling over onto her side, facing Rodrigo. Her dazzling eyes opened like precious sapphires winking back at him. His blood heated as if molten honey were being siphoned through his veins.

'*Buenos días*, beautiful...I've brought you some coffee.'

Grabbing the silk counterpane in front of her as she sat up against her pillow, she made a face. 'Not coffee. I can't stomach it at the moment, I'm afraid. But you go ahead.'

'This is because you are pregnant?' Again the immense enormity of the situation facing him hit Rodrigo.

'Yes. I haven't visited my doctor yet to confirm it, but when I return to the UK I will.'

'There's no need to wait until you return to the UK to do that. I can arrange an appointment for you to see a top obstetrician at any time, Jenny. In fact I'll get onto it as soon as we've had breakfast.'

'But don't get an appointment for today, will you?'

'Why not?' Rodrigo frowned. *Was she hiding the fact that something might be wrong?*

'Because you promised we'd visit the cathedral together today, remember? When I was here last I visited it on my own, but it wasn't the same without you.'

Her sweet dimpled smile eased his fears, and he climbed across the bed so he could join her. 'Then a promise is a promise, is it not? So we'll get ready soon and go to the cathedral. The earlier the better, as the lines of tourists form quickly. And afterwards we'll have lunch at a great restaurant I know that does fine dining.'

'We could have cheese sandwiches and a bottle of squash in the park…I really wouldn't care, Rodrigo. You don't have to impress me with fine dining.'

'I've never met another woman who was so easily satisfied.'

'Did I say anything about being easily satisfied, Señor Martinez?'

Rodrigo's stomach muscles clenched hard as iron when Jenny tugged at the drawstring on his pyjamas and then, with a warm, seductive glint in her summer-blue eyes, deliberately loosened them.

'So, you want me to show you how good I am in bed, Jenny Wren?'

She met his lowering mouth with a hungry little groan. 'Yes, please!'

CHAPTER TWELVE

IT WAS like a fairytale castle, and quite wonderful to have the chance to see it again—even more so because Rodrigo accompanied her.

As she leaned on the walking stick he'd provided Jenny gazed up at the collection of imbedded seashells in the cathedral walls, squinting in the warm early-morning sunshine to marvel at the tapering spires and curved walls, as well as the astonishing un-cathedral-like mounds of fruit that looked as if they were fashioned out of wax.

Gaudi had been a lover of nature, Rodrigo explained to her—he'd wanted to incorporate as much of nature as he could into his cathedral. Everywhere Jenny glanced was a quirky little gem, like a waterspout coming out of the mouth of a salamander or frog, and delight and awe were prevalent as she looked avidly around her. Inside, the cavernous interior was like a huge carcass that had been abandoned. But as they gazed from the walkway down at the tall cranes that were still very much part of the construction they saw that work on the Cathedral was still undoubtedly in progress. Even though the building would not be finished until around 2030 Jenny could easily imagine it filled with tall flickering pillar candles and a stunning altarpiece that the great and the good could marvel at and pay their respects.

Beside her on the walkway, Rodrigo stayed protectively close. A warm little buzz of pleasure assailed her every time she realised it. He might have experienced the cathedral many times before, but he clearly didn't take its beauty and magnificence for granted, and Jenny was certain she spent just as much time stealing furtive glances at his wonderful strong-boned profile as she did examining the stunning construction.

Leaning towards her, he whispered, 'I think it's time you took the weight off that ankle for a while. Come…we'll go back down and find a seat somewhere.'

Eschewing Jenny's idea of a simple picnic in the park, Rodrigo took her to a fabulous restaurant for lunch, which had a fleet of gleaming and expensive cars parked outside. It seemed he knew the manager well, because he was enthusiastically greeted like a long-lost friend and attention was danced upon him from the moment he and Jenny walked through the door.

Awed by the elaborate crystal chandelier twinkling above them, and the generous-sized table laid immaculately with sparkling silver cutlery overlooking a stunning white terrace, Jenny glanced down at her simple white short-sleeved blouse and aubergine-coloured skirt, praying she wasn't underdressed.

If Rodrigo's teasing sensual smile was anything to go by, she needn't have worried. Every glance he sent her way touched her like an intimate caress—as if to remind her of the passionate loving they had shared and *would* share again. And, although there were several amazing-looking women close by, having lunch with their partners or friends, it seemed he had eyes only for Jenny.

Yet as she tackled her deliciously light starter she began to feel queasy again. *This time it wasn't due to her hormones.* Why did he seem to be deliberately avoiding the topic of her pregnancy? He had asked her to give him time, but was that fair? What if he decided that he still didn't want to be with her, despite the fact they were going to have a child together? Now she didn't know if she *could* wait to have his verdict. It seemed that she'd already waited a long time for what she wanted in life.

Somewhere outside, the sound of a child's distressed crying highlighted her apprehension about the fact that her own baby's father had still not made a decision about their future.

'Rodrigo?'

'Yes, *querida*?'

'I need to talk about our situation…about what's going to happen?'

His fingers twirled the stem of his wine glass.

With a brooding expression, he lifted his gaze. 'I asked you to give me some time, did I not?'

'We don't have to get married again, if that's what you're worried about. We can still raise a child together unwed.'

But even as the words left her lips Jenny's acute sense of distress pressed in on her, like a claustrophobic bubble about to swallow her up. More than anything she'd always yearned for a family of her own. She'd waited so long to have her dream come true—had endured enough disappointment and hurt to last a lifetime. From across the table she observed Rodrigo's shuttered expression, and she couldn't help wondering if she was about to endure *more*.

'This is not easy for me,' he breathed.

'I can see that.'

His mobile phone rang. Reaching into his jacket pocket, he didn't ignore it, as Jenny had hoped he might. He spoke entirely in Spanish to the caller. She was completely excluded from the animated conversation.

When it came to an end Rodrigo leaned towards her, his air definitely distracted. 'I apologise for interrupting our meal with that call, but something has come up at the hotel that needs my attention. In fact...' he glanced down at the solid gold diver's watch that so expensively circled his tanned wrist '...I'm going to have to leave you for a while, I'm afraid. Would you mind very much if I arranged for my driver to take you back to the apartment when you've finished eating? All your needs will be catered for—you only have to ask. It's vital that I get back to the hotel for a meeting as quickly as possible.'

'You mean you're not even going to have lunch with me?'

'I'm sorry, Jenny. But this is very important.'

'And what we were just discussing *isn't*?' Crushed that he was proposing to abandon her in the restaurant to finish her lunch alone, Jenny picked up her linen napkin and threw it onto her side-plate. Searing colour scorched her cheeks as she faced him.

'Of course it's important.' Scowling in frustration, Rodrigo drummed his fingers on the table. 'But I have responsibilities—'

'Don't we all? I understand you're committed and dedicated to your job, Rodrigo—you wouldn't be such a resounding success at it if you weren't. But sometimes we have to balance our priorities, don't you think? Sometimes there are other forms of success besides work. And if the fact that in a few months' time you're going to be a father isn't a priority, then I honestly don't know what is!'

She pushed to her feet, forgetting about her still bandaged ankle, and almost lost her footing. Immediately Rodrigo came round to her side. But when he circled Jenny's waist with his arm she angrily threw him off. Right then she didn't even care if they had an audience.

'If you're leaving to go back to the hotel then I'll leave now too,' she told him, mentally garnering every bit of resolve not to cry. 'To tell you the truth, Rodrigo, I don't think I'm so keen to stay with a man who'll always put work before his personal life anyway—especially when he has a child to consider. What if our baby was ill and I needed you with me as his father, to be supportive? Would you say *Sorry, but I've got to get back to work?* Don't bother with a reply... Going by past experience I think I already know your answer.'

The Black Mercedes drew up in the private car park of the spectacular glass and chrome hotel. In the elegant, luxurious confines that separated them from the driver, Rodrigo tugged Jenny's pale slim hand onto his lap. His expression was racked and conflicted, she saw.

'Do you know how bad I feel about leaving you like this?'

'If you feel so bad then you'll postpone your meeting...at least for a couple of hours...so we can talk,' Jenny returned reasonably.

Scraping his fingers through his ebony mane, Rodrigo emitted a long frustrated sigh. 'I'm afraid that's impossible.'

'Impossible meaning you can't postpone it, or you *won't*?'

'*Dios mio!* An extraordinary meeting has been urgently called, with half a dozen shareholders waiting on my decision about a considerable financial undertaking for the hotel, and I absolutely *cannot* postpone it. Initially I instructed my second-in-command to stand in for me, but when I spoke to him at lunch I realised he was not as fully informed about the deal as I am. I'm genuinely sorry about this, *querida*, but we will talk as long as you want when I return. I promise you.'

With a quick kiss on her cheek, and the drift of his tantalising cologne lingering in the space he'd left behind, Rodrigo knocked on the glass partition to give some instructions to his driver and in a flash… was gone.

Never before had he endured such hard-to-bear impatience. It was like torture. As his driver weaved the car through the converging traffic, with furious horns being honked loudly and drivers gesticulating wildly, Rodrigo almost…*almost* wanted to get out and walk back to the apartment.

For about the hundredth time he checked the time on his watch. Leaving his delighted shareholders toasting him with champagne after the mutually satisfying outcome of the meeting—as well as the extremely healthy financial report his accountant had given them—he'd all but knocked them over to get out of the boardroom.

Dragging his tie away from his shirt collar, he glanced out of the tinted car windows and gritted his teeth. *All he wanted to do now was get back to Jenny.* He should have postponed the meeting. His portfolio and kudos were such that he could have easily put it off until it was more convenient. Now, remembering Jenny's disbelieving face and angry declaration that she wasn't so keen any more to be with a man who put his work first, Rodrigo wished he *had*. Oh, why had he messed up again when he'd been given an incredible second chance to make things right?

A sight suddenly transfixed him. The car had purred to a stop to let a small family cross the road in front of them. There was an older woman, with a red tint in her hair, and a pretty young couple with a baby. All three of them were fussing and cooing over the infant, until Rodrigo's driver beeped on his horn to indicate to them that they could safely cross, and suddenly Rodrigo was deluged by his need to hold Jenny close and confess his adoration and love for her—to make her see how sorry he was for being such an idiot.

Why on earth had it taken him so long to realise what a precious jewel he had in his grasp? Had he been blind? What if after this new disappointment she completely gave up on him and left him for good? Although it was totally his own fault, he didn't think he could bear it. She was carrying his baby, and—given the chance—he *would* be the supportive father she yearned for him to be. Never again would he put some damn board meeting before *her*. Somewhere along the line he'd lost perspective. Being a success in business had become like a runaway train.

Rapping on the glass partition, he spoke rapidly to his driver, opened the passenger door and leapt out.

With his heart pounding and the sweat sticking his shirt like glue to his back in the sultry afternoon sun he sprinted hard all the way back to the apartment.

She was gone. With mounting shock Rodrigo found the bedroom empty of all her baggage and belongings. The luxurious apartment had never felt so lonely or so empty—apart from the first time Jenny had left, that was.

With a despairing oath he prowled the rooms, searching for clues that might tell him where she'd gone. There wasn't even a note. However, he did find a scrap of paper with her address and telephone number back in the UK written hastily on it, left poignantly on his pillow.

Hardly daring even to mentally articulate the conclusion that was rapidly forming in his mind, he rang the concierge to have his worst fears confirmed: Jenny had indeed ordered a cab to take her to the airport…

Thankfully the airport manager had been a fantastic help. He'd had to waive quite a few airport regulations to get Rodrigo as far as the passenger lounge where customers waited before boarding their flights. Now, with his impatient gaze scanning the sea of heads, he felt his heartbeat almost career to a standstill when he spied Jenny on a seat at the back, in deep conversation with a young, curly-haired youth dressed very casually in baggy denims and an equally baggy sweatshirt.

Rodrigo straightened his silk tie and stole a couple of moments in which to compose himself. His heart was still pounding. Suddenly, as if she'd sensed his presence, Jenny glanced up, her gaze colliding in astonishment with his.

Moving to stand in front of her, he felt the words he so desperately wanted to say die on his lips as he glanced avidly into her stunning summer-blue eyes.

'Forgive me,' he finally breathed. 'I've been such an idiot! I should never have gone to that meeting instead of staying and talking to you.'

'What are you—what are you doing here, Rodrigo?'

He grimaced. 'More to the point, *mi angel*...what are *you* doing here?'

She dipped her head. 'I'm flying home. I would willingly walk through fire for you, Rodrigo, but I won't stay around where I'm not wanted. When I saw that you were quite willing to leave me alone at lunch and go to a meeting, I realised that it was no different from the first time we were together. It's your business that means the world to you...not me or our baby. I'm afraid that Barcelona suddenly lost its charm.' She swallowed hard. 'When I get home we can discuss things on the phone. I left my number on your pillow.'

'You would walk through fire for me, you said?'

'I love you. Didn't you know that?'

With a racing heart, Rodrigo dropped down into the shiny hard chair next to her. When the curly-haired young man Jenny had been talking to openly stared at him he pierced him with a steely gaze and said, 'Do you mind? I'm having a private conversation with my fiancée.'

Jenny gulped, pressing her hand against her heart. 'What did you say?'

'Wait a moment. I want to do this properly, Jenny Wren.'

To her utter amazement, Rodrigo dropped down onto his bended knee in front of her. Several heads in the lounge's vicinity swivelled interestedly. Reaching for her hand, he raised it to his lips. The warmth of his mouth made her insides dissolve as surely as ice cream beneath a blazing sun. 'Will you marry me Jenny—and this time for good? Marry me and make me happier than I'm sure I deserve.' Removing the solid gold signet ring from the little finger on his left hand, he slid it onto Jenny's wedding finger.

'Are you serious, Rodrigo?' She couldn't help the husky catch in her voice. The whole scenario was overwhelming…*surreal*, even.

'More serious than I've ever been about anything in my life,' he answered, grinning. 'The business has always meant a lot to me…I don't deny that. My father drummed it into me from a young age that I should strive to make a name for myself in business…

that I should work hard and not be distracted from my focus. Not even if I fell in love. But the dream of success he sold to me was *his*, not mine. My mother was the wise one, but it took me until today to realize just *how* wise. She wanted me to have a family, Jenny. She told me it was the most important thing and she was right. And even though her relationship with my father was not exactly made in heaven she believed in the legacy of a loving family with all her heart. Now my own feelings echo that. You and our baby mean the world to me and I will always endeavour to put you both first…I swear it.'

'Do you mean that?' As she bent down to whisper the question, Jenny found her lips captured eagerly and hungrily, and for long moments she forgot everything but the sensation of the delicious pressure of Rodrigo's passionate mouth on hers.

Drawing away from him after a while, she was shocked to hear the steady resounding echo of applause in her ears. Several people were on their feet in support, and when Rodrigo also got to his feet he winked at Jenny, then turned to give their audience a highly theatrical bow.

As he pulled her back into his arms she gazed up eagerly into his loving dark eyes and smiled. 'I reckon that wild storm *did* bring you to me that night, Rodrigo. It took me a while to believe that fate had brought you back…given us a second chance…but now I don't doubt it. I'm just so grateful, my love.'

'And I echo the words I told you then… My body, my heart and my soul are yours for ever, my bewitching Jenny Wren. I pray you never have cause to doubt it, but I swear I will spend the rest of my life showing you how ardent I am!'

SEPTEMBER 2010 HARDBACK TITLES

ROMANCE

A Stormy Greek Marriage	Lynne Graham
Unworldly Secretary, Untamed Greek	Kim Lawrence
The Sabbides Secret Baby	Jacqueline Baird
The Undoing of de Luca	Kate Hewitt
Katrakis's Last Mistress	Caitlin Crews
Surrender to Her Spanish Husband	Maggie Cox
Passion, Purity and the Prince	Annie West
For Revenge or Redemption?	Elizabeth Power
Red Wine and Her Sexy Ex	Kate Hardy
Every Girl's Secret Fantasy	Robyn Grady
Cattle Baron Needs a Bride	Margaret Way
Passionate Chef, Ice Queen Boss	Jennie Adams
Sparks Fly with Mr Mayor	Teresa Carpenter
Rescued in a Wedding Dress	Cara Colter
Wedding Date with the Best Man	Melissa McClone
Maid for the Single Dad	Susan Meier
Alessandro and the Cheery Nanny	Amy Andrews
Valentino's Pregnancy Bombshell	Amy Andrews

HISTORICAL

Reawakening Miss Calverley	Sylvia Andrew
The Unmasking of a Lady	Emily May
Captured by the Warrior	Meriel Fuller

MEDICAL™

Dating the Millionaire Doctor	Marion Lennox
A Knight for Nurse Hart	Laura Iding
A Nurse to Tame the Playboy	Maggie Kingsley
Village Midwife, Blushing Bride	Gill Sanderson

0810 Gen Std LP

SEPTEMBER 2010 LARGE PRINT TITLES

ROMANCE

Virgin on Her Wedding Night	Lynne Graham
Blackwolf's Redemption	Sandra Marton
The Shy Bride	Lucy Monroe
Penniless and Purchased	Julia James
Beauty and the Reclusive Prince	Raye Morgan
Executive: Expecting Tiny Twins	Barbara Hannay
A Wedding at Leopard Tree Lodge	Liz Fielding
Three Times A Bridesmaid...	Nicola Marsh

HISTORICAL

The Viscount's Unconventional Bride	Mary Nichols
Compromising Miss Milton	Michelle Styles
Forbidden Lady	Anne Herries

MEDICAL™

The Doctor's Lost-and-Found Bride	Kate Hardy
Miracle: Marriage Reunited	Anne Fraser
A Mother for Matilda	Amy Andrews
The Boss and Nurse Albright	Lynne Marshall
New Surgeon at Ashvale A&E	Joanna Neil
Desert King, Doctor Daddy	Meredith Webber

MILLS & BOON

OCTOBER 2010 HARDBACK TITLES

ROMANCE

The Reluctant Surrender	Penny Jordan
Shameful Secret, Shotgun Wedding	Sharon Kendrick
The Virgin's Choice	Jennie Lucas
Scandal: Unclaimed Love-Child	Melanie Milburne
Powerful Greek, Housekeeper Wife	Robyn Donald
Hired by Her Husband	Anne McAllister
Snowbound Seduction	Helen Brooks
A Mistake, A Prince and A Pregnancy	Maisey Yates
Champagne with a Celebrity	Kate Hardy
When He was Bad...	Anne Oliver
Accidentally Pregnant!	Rebecca Winters
Star-Crossed Sweethearts	Jackie Braun
A Miracle for His Secret Son	Barbara Hannay
Proud Rancher, Precious Bundle	Donna Alward
Cowgirl Makes Three	Myrna Mackenzie
Secret Prince, Instant Daddy!	Raye Morgan
Officer, Surgeon...Gentleman!	Janice Lynn
Midwife in the Family Way	Fiona McArthur

HISTORICAL

Innocent Courtesan to Adventurer's Bride	Louise Allen
Disgrace and Desire	Sarah Mallory
The Viking's Captive Princess	Michelle Styles

MEDICAL™

Bachelor of the Baby Ward	Meredith Webber
Fairytale on the Children's Ward	Meredith Webber
Playboy Under the Mistletoe	Joanna Neil
Their Marriage Miracle	Sue MacKay

0910 Gen Std LP

OCTOBER 2010 LARGE PRINT TITLES

ROMANCE

Marriage: To Claim His Twins	Penny Jordan
The Royal Baby Revelation	Sharon Kendrick
Under the Spaniard's Lock and Key	Kim Lawrence
Sweet Surrender with the Millionaire	Helen Brooks
Miracle for the Girl Next Door	Rebecca Winters
Mother of the Bride	Caroline Anderson
What's A Housekeeper To Do?	Jennie Adams
Tipping the Waitress with Diamonds	Nina Harrington

HISTORICAL

Practical Widow to Passionate Mistress	Louise Allen
Major Westhaven's Unwilling Ward	Emily Bascom
Her Banished Lord	Carol Townend

MEDICAL™

The Nurse's Brooding Boss	Laura Iding
Emergency Doctor and Cinderella	Melanie Milburne
City Surgeon, Small Town Miracle	Marion Lennox
Bachelor Dad, Girl Next Door	Sharon Archer
A Baby for the Flying Doctor	Lucy Clark
Nurse, Nanny...Bride!	Alison Roberts